James Everett Kibler

Memory's Keep

Books by James Everett Kibler

Our Fathers' Fields: A Southern Story
Child to the Waters
Walking Toward Home
Memory's Keep

Memory's Keep

James Everett Kibler

PELICAN PUBLISHING COMPANY
Gretna 2006

*The word "Pelican" and the depiction of a pelican
are trademarks of Pelican Publishing Company, Inc.,
and are registered in the U.S. Patent and Trademark Office.*

Library of Congress Cataloging-in-Publication Data

Kibler, James E.
  Memory's keep / James Everett Kibler.
    p. cm.
  ISBN-13: 978-1-58980-371-8 (hardcover : alk. paper)
  1. Southern States—Fiction. 2. Widower—Fiction. 3.
Farm life—Fiction. I. Title.
  PS3611.I26M46 2006
  813'.54—dc22
2006014751

This is a work of fiction. Any resemblance to actual living persons or events is coincidental.

Printed in the United States of America

Published by Pelican Publishing Company, Inc.
1000 Burmaster Street, Gretna, Louisiana 70053

To the memory of my mother,
Juanita Connelly Kibler (21 November 1921-1 October 2004)

Contents

Preface

Memory's Keep can be read on its own. It has a beginning and end, but it's also the second volume of my Clay Bank County series begun with *Walking Toward Home*. When I finished that first work in 2003, I had more questions about the characters than that novel had answered. One of the leading ones was, "Why on earth is Trig Tinsley such an independent cuss? . . . What has led him to be such a 'one-of-a-kind' in a 'one-size-fits-all' world?" Everyone in the first novel realises Trig has achieved that much-honoured status of the Character. He's already become a legend that way when we first meet him there.

We in the South love our Characters. That fact says much about our tolerance and valuing of individuality. We take pride in them at the same time we may not be brave enough to resist conforming ourselves. The more we conform, the more we love our Characters.

"Oh, how sad!" we're always saying. "All the Characters are dying out." We regret the fact, but just as we've thought that the last one has passed from the scene, other folks in our acquaintance quite unexpectedly start exhibiting traits and behaviour for which there just doesn't seem to be any good reason at all. Soon, some of these folks are well on their way to becoming Characters as unique as those who went before, and the genus *curmudgeon* is preserved.

Memory's Keep takes Trig back more than twenty-five years in time, to the mid-1970s, when he's a young man in his twenties making the choices and gaining the experiences that will make him who he is in *Walking Toward Home*. That first volume, set in 2003, had introduced us to three friends, given equal time: Chauncey, Kildee, and Trig, all quite different personalities—a kind of id, ego, superego sort of a thing—but with place and values in common too. This second volume, however, is Trig's.

So then *Memory's Keep* is a flashback, within which we go even deeper in time—in fact, over a century and a half deeper. Pull a Southern thread, and the whole unravels, to be rewoven again in a sturdier fabric. Everything connects and leads both backward and onward at one and the same time. In the rewoven creation, both design and pattern are there, but still not ever quite clearly revealed. Such is life—the unsolvable mystery that it is.

Like the keep of a castle, the memory is the most interior and sacred of places, the inviolate, unassailable centre that best protects our humanity and says who we are. Scientists don't like memory very much. It's the province of art, and, in an age when science has come to dominate, it must be defended above all. Momentary man, living for the gratification of the now, doesn't care much for memories. He finds them instead a threat, an inconvenience, and a hindrance besides—something inefficient and impractical, and best to be rid of. The folks of the Clay Bank County series, whatever their shortcomings, are not momentary women and men. Provincials of place, they might certainly be, but never provincials of time. They do not inhabit a throwaway world.

Memory's Keep

I

Mister Pink
~∾~

Mister Pink sat on the porch of the old house. Now a weathered grey, it hadn't been painted for well over a century, probably not since before the war, as people around these parts still referred to the era of the 1850s. Then came the war itself, with the loss of so many men in four hard years of conflict and the resulting gradual collapse of the farming economy, given its final coup in the 1930s and '40s. All had been connected events that brought the old man to this place and spot in time. 30 July 1975. A bright summer day. He sat on his porch alone.

Of late, Mister Pink had been thinking more and more of old times. He would better remember what happened to him or was told him as a little lad than what had taken place just yesterday. Old folks had said that's what it would be like with memory when you got their age, and now he knew they were telling him true.

His pa and ma had been slaves on this very land. Its geography was all Mister Pink knew—a rich, high, flat bluff along the Broad River, a thickly wooded plateau that dropped off precipitously, and ran down to a flood plain that was incredibly rich and made the very best sweet potatoes and corn.

The natives, before the white man came, called the big stream *Eswapudeenah,* meaning the boundary between the hunting grounds of Catawba and Cherokee. The land where Pink lived was on the Cherokee side. He found evidences of them in the arrowheads that looked like giant teeth—and in little pieces of clay pottery he turned up with his plough. From the time he was a boy, he thought about the presence of these ancient people on the ground he walked and hoed. Sometimes they seemed to be talking to him when the wind passed through the trees.

Pink's pa was a master teller of stories in a land known for this gift. In a time that was demanding flat statement and statistics, Mister Pink had still tried to teach his children that way, though they often got impatient with him.

Mister Pink had a rich fund of history, the gift of his pa, an eyewitness to stirring big times. Mister Pink remembered that his pa was serene in old age because during his day, he'd faced about every sort of desperate trouble a man could imagine and had still survived. There was no terror left that could try him at all. Yes, Pink remembered well.

Better than statistics, his pa's stories told who they were. The stories would abide longer too than any casual fact. The people here would be revealed and known, not so much by statements, but by the stories they told and how they were told, and what they chose as important to tell. These were the registers that finally mattered most in the big span of things.

In Pink's father's day, the young master, whose name was Berry Richards and whose land it would have become, had been killed in the last battle of the Virginia campaign. Pink's pa had been with Richards as his body servant, cooking for the two of them and caring for their horses, and at times shouldering a rifle too. Dutiful to the last, his final act in caring for his master's person was to bring the empty shell of it home to the young missus and their two little girls.

Berry Richards and Pink's pa had been born on the same day in 1839. Mr. Richards made much of the fact, and when the lads were old enough to understand the solemn nature of the ritual, he gave Pink's pa to his son, saying, as Pink's pa often recounted, "Suber, you belongs to Marse Berry now. Y'all are bonded for all time."

And so it was. Suber and Berry were devoted playmates, engaging in the usual horseplay of children and growing up together in a precious time of plenty and no hunger or want. Suber used to tell Pink about their games of acting horse and mule on all fours, each child riding the other in turn, on the deep wool plush of fine rose-figured Belgian carpets, or the cool velvet smooth of bright Aubusson weave, while the old master would sit in his great brocaded armchair by the deep hearth and guffaw.

It was a capacious time. Old Master and Missus would raise their cut crystal stem glasses and smile and wink at the lads as they sipped. The firelight made the sherry a rich golden red, the colour of the old master's favourite roan mare, Guenevere.

Death broke the bond, Marse Berry getting hit with the invader's lead full square in the right shoulder so as nearly to sunder it from the trunk and with such velocity as to spin him halfway around. The blood spattered Suber's own coat, so close they were. For all his doing, Suber couldn't stop the scarlet flow, and his master died there on the battlefield where Suber had pulled him beneath the shelter of a giant walnut tree.

Suber's mind must have gone blank in the shock and agony of all this, and the battle's din, for when dark came and the gleaners of the scene of carnage came to take away those who were still groaning and wailing in pain, Suber, by the side of his master realised the whole right shoulder and back of his grey wool coat was cold and stiff with his master's blood. At some time during his getting him to safety, he must have put him over his shoulder to carry him. He never even recollected doing this though. Next thing he knew he was sitting with his back to the tree, crying like a little child.

Suber brought him home, and now Richards' grave had its modest marble marker, shrunken small by the poverty and desolation of all around in that time. Still, as was the custom of the countryside, the important thing was that the grave, fancy or plain or indeed unmarked, faced east; and from off its high bluff, one could easily picture the last day when the first streaks of dawn would come across the grey mirror-slick river and illumine the faces of the resurrected, the flawed flesh burned away in its frailness and replaced by the incorruptible form.

Suber had now taken his place there as well, still at his master's side, a large fieldstone marking his head, and a small one his feet—with his grave also facing east to the rising sun. At certain times, when a slant of light fell a certain way through the thick covering of trees that sheltered these graves, the mica and quartz in Suber's stone shone like a thousand diamonds, and the carved rose on Richards' marble marker glowed as if from within.

Mister Pink often visited these lonely plots there on this part of the windy high river bluff within sight of the old house, and thought how it might be in the end, when his pa and Marse Berry would rise and regard one another with a long look of satisfaction of things well done and complete, before taking their own flights on wings of silver and gold. It was something important to keep one's bond, maybe the essential thing. Yes, that and the duty of man to be just, forgiving, and to walk humbly before his God.

Mister Pink thought long and long about all this, and about this ragged out old place, so fallen into disrepair and ruin, and of the collapse and inevitable decay of things.

Born close to two decades after the war, Mister Pink knew more than a little about the way things went to smash around here. Ruin and the death of young Berry killed the old master prematurely, and his wife soon followed behind. Berry's widow and the two girls lost the homeplace, and the young missus remarrying, they all moved away, far across the great river to a place Mister Pink did not know.

They and their descendants had all vanished now, never to be seen again, like even the living were gone from the very face of the earth. For Mister Pink, they moved into the dark void, a nameless empty region like his idea of death.

Suber and his wife Mamie Lou, and Pink's seven siblings, stayed on as tenants of new owners, who were not from these parts and lived in town. They were city folks by birth and inclination, from the North, coming South seeking cheap real estate and escaping the cold. They took up land as a diversion, having bought the acres in a bargain, as they thought, from a forced tax sale on the courthouse steps. The place had thus passed out of the Richards family name. These new owners had in turn sold the place to friends from back home, as they themselves moved on farther South, following the sun.

Mister Pink didn't see much of any of these new folks. They came around only to get their portion share of what Suber and his family raised, and the best of their salt-cured hams, which they particularly relished as centerpieces for their dinner parties and each year's big Christmas affair. Vegetables of Pink's make, they'd declare to their town neighbours, to be "fresh from the farm." Otherwise, the new ones took little interest. They left their tenants to their own devices, and Suber and Mamie Lou finally preferred it that way.

All was friendly enough, but in a formal business manner. Mamie Lou tried to soften the situation with gifts of a peach cobbler, a pecan or blackberry pie, with berries picked by the children out of the snake-haunted thickets from off the land; but still there was the distance, like across a gully or in a deep well. Suber, who had no last name when the war came to an end, had to have a surname to attach to tax and tenantry documents. So, close by the X of his mark, he had the clerk write "Suber," thus making his first name his last. He left it at that and never chose a Christian first name, though he'd been taught Scripture by old Master and Miss. With this, they had taken pains.

So what would have been his son's just plain Pink in slave days became Pink Suber in times after the war.

Pink was a tall, strong-limbed fellow, whose skin had the blue-black sheen of coal. The harsh, hardscrabble nature of the times had sometimes made his eyes as hard as coal too. Still they were alert eyes that didn't miss much. They had to be, he knew, if he was to survive. And his gentle, pleasant nature stood him in good stead and softened his life. He was a good, careful, hardworking farmer, and he and his wife Goldie relished the life.

Indeed, it was all that he and Goldie knew, but they'd gained wisdom deep enough to view labour, the details and discipline of it, as purifying ritual. Digging, ploughing, hoeing, chopping, harvesting, butchering, sawing, sewing, mending, quilting—there was a kind of primitive drama in all this necessity that brought catharsis besides. Sweat from hard work was a kind of baptism too.

Today though, Mister Pink sat at rest on a straight

chair, stained blue with copperas and indigo dye. He'd cut the poplar and oak for the chair from the woods himself, turned the posts with his own lathe, and caned its bottom with long split white oak splints he drew from the moist, fragrant wood with his drawing knife.

There on the warp-boarded floor of the porch and beneath the triangle of its grey-weathered classical pediment, he would sit at dusk. This time every day, you could count on him there.

From the vantage of the old porch, he had a lot of time to consider things. His world was mainly the sweeping arc of great white oaks that fanned out as the semicircular carriage drive in former days, arching out in front of the house.

Their giant dark limbs were larger than a big man's torso, and on them grew the delicate tendrils of resurrection ferns. During the dry spells of July and August, the ferns appeared completely dead. Their fronds shrivelled, drawn up like bows; but brown as they were, it would only take a shower or a good morning fog in the coming fall to revive and unfurl them and turn them a luxuriant and emerald green. They cheered grey winter days with their freshness.

The old carriage building, a little temple itself, stood nearby in a grove of rowan and ash trees, its design echoing the classical lines in miniature of the dwelling house itself. The days of carriages were done, and Mister Pink had no money for a car. He walked everywhere he went, which was seldom and not far. In all his days, he'd never left the county, or wished very much to. Someone asked him if he didn't want to view the broad sea. It wasn't but a four-hour's drive away. His answer was simple and brief. "If the Lord wills it, I'll see it in heaven."

With the roof of the carriage building gone, the structure was quickly dissolving back into the ground from which it had arisen like a dream. A column lay fallen to one side on the ground. Another still clung akimbo to the cornice frieze. Giant honeysuckle vines and Virginia creeper had long been engulfing its walls and hastening the wood's decay. In spring, the honeysuckle perfumed the air; in the late fall, the burgundy red of the splayed leaves of creeper lent bright beauty to the wood's grey.

Pink's pa had told him that the rowan trees had been planted by the old master himself. The Richards kin in the mother country had known them to be a protection against evil, and the family carried the tradition into the new land.

All the rest of Mister Pink's view from his blue chair was sparse fields and mostly forest. Each year that rolled round, the field plots shrank in size, as the woods grew taller and darker, deeper and closer too. As the strength gradually left his limbs and his will to do waned, wild nature seemed to be reclaiming its own. It was slowly, but surely, approaching his door.

There was that old, inexorable tug of the land, the very soil itself, or something deep buried at the core inside, that kept on beckoning to Pink to come and lie down in it, to sleep long, a long winter's sleep. Sometimes it sang him a deep earth song.

Goldie had died three years ago and long before that, all their children had long since moved away to various far distant cities he'd only heard of or dreamed of in sleep. Now, he was alone in a silent world whose deep woods got nearer and nearer and whose soil spoke each year with a louder and more distinct voice. Pink had begun to imagine it had now taken to calling him by name. *Pink. Pink Suber. Pink. Come lie down and rest.* Its tone had got more insistent these days.

Perhaps one not born of this place would fail to understand the curious air of dilapidation that lay over Mister Pink's world. At first maybe his impulse might be to hustle in and feverishly clean and tidy things up. He might work and work until his very soul cried out. Then, his mission accomplished, and straightening his back, he would look around with an expression of delight to think he had shaped things to his liking, had conquered the wildness of the country, brought it under his iron will. But how quickly that expression would vanish, would change to bewilderment straight. True, the stranger had been told by those longer and wiser on the land—those folks like Mister Pink himself—that the minute he'd turn his back on this tidied up world, it would return to its quiet disorder, its lush rank growth and mellow decay. But the stranger not bred to the rhythm of this place just thought this was local talk and local laziness—an excuse not to be bustling about and doing.

But now with some experience and wisdom, the stranger would learn that indeed this was not just talk, for he soon comprehended that born in the body, and bred in the inexorable bare bone of this land was always an air of transience, of the passing and fleeting, and that this same flux of slow time suffused all.

Here great trees fell, their rotted skeletons soon to be host to man-tall cinnamon ferns. Smaller shield and autumn and hay-scented ferns grew in their shade. Thick mosses grew; books mildewed, their leather bindings warping beyond repair; gravestones weathered, crumbled, and turned lichen-grey. No paint would ever stay on any wood; no vines ever give up their tindreled hold. The very clapboards themselves would warp and pull through their nails from house's frame. Brick walls, seemingly so solid, would ooze wet, and plaster walls crack and crumble with moisture, run and drip. Earthworms would digest their velvet fare in the rich fall of leaves. A leaf drifted down, and silent forces at once began gathering it in.

It was simply a place too fertile for the hands and will of man to shape and keep penned within man-imposed bounds. Things grew too rapidly for that in an almost yearlong growing season; there was no white frozen landscape to aid man's proscription and keep life tidy and its process at bay.

Here in Mister Pink's world, and for Mister Pink himself, wisdom brought the realisation that existence was not tidy, and its deep nature would never be. This was a truth not to be seen so easily on asphalt and concrete, of which Mister Pink knew next to none.

Indeed, Pink was born to this deeper understanding and did not have to be told. As in the land itself, it was born in his body, bred in his bone. He took life as it came and did not beat against the incoming tide, for the tide brought myriad life in its unfathomable deep brine.

He had no illusions about modern times and its much-vaunted progress. He was once heard to say that with every advancement, there's an equal or greater backpeddling in time. Of modern gains, he'd often declare, "Improvements makes straight fast roads, but it's by the crooked roads that's the best places to live." He'd learned in his life that it was usually by the winding and indirect paths that he'd found his way. He expected it to be the same way with mankind.

This day on his cane-bottomed chair, he had near fallen into a drowse. The hazy spell of memory was upon him, and in these moments, he didn't like much to be disturbed.

A line of sandhill cranes lazily flew their way westward with the river as guide. They moved in ragged, but determined style, their line moving up and down like waves at sea. They looked at ease with the world. Contented, Pink followed the familiar sight with practised eye.

Few could get away with breaking Mister Pink's reverie and drowse, but one was Preacher Jones. Not that the Reverend often came this way or that Mister Pink had any great love of him or the church he lorded over like emperor or king.

Goldie had been big in the church, sang in the choir, and perhaps this was one reason that Reverend Jones was making his call. Another no doubt was his recollection of

Mister Pink's quality hams, true excellence in a community that knew hams.

Reverend Jones was a big man, impressively big, with a large girth of paunch to match his height. Truth to say, he carried his weight well. He had on his Sunday-go-to-meeting best, and sported a pink shirt and big rhinestone pin as a tie tac on his plum-purple tie. Of the splendidness of this, Mister Pink made his usual note.

A gold eyetooth glinted each time the Reverend spoke or smiled. He drove a big shiny black Cadillac car. Its engine's roar and the tires' scrape on the hard rutted red clay announced his arrival with fanfare that would have been appropriate for a modern-day Caesar.

Reverend Jones lost no time in steering the conversation round to the topic he was most interested in.

"Pink, is that a smokehouse I sees back behind them big popular trees?"

"Yessir, Preacher, you've said true. You got eagle eyes."

"Bet that smokehouse has plenty of prime cured hams."

"Not so many as when my Goldie was here, but I always still butchers me my share of hogs in butchering time. I likes to have a-plenty at Christmas, when the chaps all visits me here."

"Lucky chilrens. Bet your hams are the best around. My mouth waters just at the thought and a mention of them."

Well, this conversation didn't take the route the Reverend tried, nor ended at the intended destination. At the preacher's last comment, Pink stayed silent, and watched the great black and white pileated woodpecker dip heavily across the cirque of giant trees in front of them. Its raucous call startled and changed the subject complete.

The Reverend soon scraped chair and was gone, leaving a powdering of dust from his car wheels. Mister Pink returned to his reverie again. The preacher had gotten no hams.

The car's dust reminded him of his father's favourite saying of dry spells like these. "Rather feel the mud 'tween my toes than the dust up my nose," he'd say of a drought. Pink mused on his pa and ma as he'd known them in the pride of their strength. Then his thought drifted back to the undulating line of cranes he'd seen before Reverend Jones had come, and he fell back to his musing.

Finally, breaking from his drowse and sandhill crane reverie, Pink *harrumphed* once or twice and finally broke silence with words that addressed the air around.

"One thing for sure, like taxes and death. Preacher Jones won't get no ham from me, lessen he puts his footses under my table here."

But Reverend Jones was not likely to do that. He held himself higher than Pink, a mighty man in the world, and had city-folks' ways. Ham or no ham, he'd not settle so low.

The red sun was brooding heavy with the summer heat and was drooping now in the west across a scraggly half-harvested peanut patch and the bedraggled line of spindly stalks of okra with their hibiscus-like bloom. Funny how from such a stark and leafless, dried-up cane, the exotic cream yellow flowers blossomed. They opened wide, revealing their dark purple eye, lasted a day, and fell. Here again was the spendthrift nature of this land, this rag-tag forgotten land of the precious and few. Where the yellow blossom had been, a green nub formed, then the miraculous emerald pod. It elongated and grew big in the space of a day.

The fig trees in the yard were heavy with fruit. Sugar dripped from the bud end of them in their fecundness. The little red openings wept like eyes.

Not like that fig tree Scripture tells us about, that wouldn't give nothing to our hungry Lord, Pink thought. *And Him on his way to die too and needin' all the strength he could get, knowin' what he was about to have to do. I'd shorely bloomed into fruit, if I'd 'a been that tree. When you're needed that way, there's no good reason to wait.*

Pink watched the redbirds fly in and out of the fig trees' cool green recesses, greedily slashing the ripe brown jackets with their sharp yellow beaks so that the fruit hung down in red tatters and shreds like torn and defeated flags.

Reminded by the Reverend's talk of food, and the greedily feeding birds, Mister Pink bethought him of ham, and grits and redeye gravy too, all easy to cook up in a simple supper, and easier to eat. Tonight with the biscuits he'd baked this morning, he'd have honey in the comb, taken just yesterday from a hive of his bees in the sourwood trees.

But first he'd just watch the unfolding play of the sun's display, with its saffrons and purples and lemon yellows and lavenders and shades of rose, and a coral light pink he'd seen only in the insides of a giant seashell (a conch they called it) brought back two hundred miles from the sea by Marse Richards in the golden old days, as Pink's pa had told, and which still sat on the floor at the many-lighted transom and sidelights that surrounded the old house's heavy double front doors.

Some of the little diamond-shaped panes were now gone, and Pink had stuffed rags in the spaces to keep out the cold, but the dying sun caught the wavy, hand-poured crystalline glass of the panes that remained and irradiated the gloom of the deep hall behind. It lit up the levitation of dust motes that hung thickly and frozen as if by magic in its still air.

There in the shadows of the wide cool hall and into what had once been the drawing room, Pink had strung a crisscross of clotheslines for his pitiful plain garments, grown thin and soft from many washings in the big black iron pot outside, and which now hung crazily in lines like soldiers scattered in rout after fierce enemy assault.

Now the sun's bottom rim just fell below the tree line; and taking that as a direct cue and sign, Mister Pink bestirred himself to come inside, marking the conclusion of yet another day. As it always began, so it ended, with Pink giving heartfelt thanks to his Maker for being able still to move and breathe and be, taking one day at a time.

"The sun is God's own candle. When He puts it out, He rests for awhile, like we does after a long day's work in the field," Mister Pink said aloud. "One day He'll put me out too, but only to light me again."

The mumble of his words sounded in rhythmical even-song accompaniment to the *taptaptaptap* of his stout, hand-whittled cane on the bone-dry boards of the old porch floor. After a good day's labour, it was painful for him now just to straighten himself out and walk.

"Going home," Mister Pink said, as he entered the heavy door that shut behind him with a creak and slam. It had the sound of finality that echoed to the depths of the great empty hall.

Then suddenly from the orange west, the diamond panes of the transom caught fire from a ray of the sun's last coppery radiance and just for a brief moment made all the hall full and golden with light.

"My soul is lit by the lantern of God," Mister Pink said in salute and reply.

His clothes hanging there in the hall on the chaos of lines moved uneasily in the draft of the closing door, which also made the dust motes fly as leaves before a great storm. To Mister Pink, the empty clothes were like the ghosts of all of those gone before. There was his pa and ma, and the young master who lay buried on the windswept hill, a man he'd never seen, leastways in life, and the old master and missus before him, stepping out of deep legend and oft-repeated tale.

The golden light faded away into gloom, and was quickly gone, as if never there. The clothes returned to being clothes, needed taking down, folding, and putting away. He'd wait till tomorrow to do them. Now supper needed making, and preparations for night.

Here, in what the old people used to call early candle-lighting time, Pink would eat his modest repast and commune once again with this legion of the dead, made palpable present in all that he touched, smelled, and saw, so that his final question would always recur to him as he drifted to doze in his chair by the hearth: "Who then are the living, and who the dead? God fixin' to take me, and then I will know." But for now, Mister Pink knew that the deep central mystery would remain.

II

Old Stephney

The moaning came piercingly sharp through the evening air. It was Chellie. Her voice was recognisable through the depths of pain. The last three days had been a trial few had ever witnessed before. The men in blue who'd invaded their land had come over fifty thousand strong to their fields and homes and laid everything waste. What the soldiers could not carry away, they destroyed. The soil lay bare and scorched. Old Dove, the only mule left on the place because she was too old to be worth stealing, lay dead. Her cut throat ran a black puddle of blood on the charred ground. Several of the little children gathered around her with teary eyes. Their faithful old hound lay dead nearby under a cape jessamine bush, a ball through his head.

The Richards family had lost all. The slaves had the same. All their food was gone, and now what were they to do? The black men were barefooted. The soldiers had even taken their shoes. They sat about their desolate dwellings as if shell-shocked—a quiet island in the thick of war.

They appealed to old Master and Miss, but they too were in shock, their eyes blasted by the recent death in battle of Berry, their only son.

And the moaning kept coming, never keener, never lighter, just the same, in an even high wail, and with no letup at all. There Chellie sat on the wooden steps of her one-room cabin, swaying back and forth and making that sound.

It was only last week that her infant daughter had died, prematurely born from its mother's fear, anxiety, and fatigue. Without even enough time for giving her a name, they had buried her in a little wooden box, and Chellie had cried.

Now, the men in blue, in their search for valuables, had tried every new-dug spot of ground. They had uncovered the pine box, knocked it open, and left the poor babe.

So Chellie moaned, with a depth of pain that soaked into the melancholy land, making it tragic indeed. Her wails seemed to melt into the surroundings, her swayings into the motion of tall trees.

"What kinds of men dig up a chile and leave her for de hog to root? What kinds of men?" was all she could say through her sobs, for, indeed, it was just luck that she and the others had found the poor babe before the farm animals did.

The sky was dark with ashes from the burning barns and outbuildings. The sun would not show its face and look on the scene.

"Oh Lawd, precious Lawd," she lamented to the smoky sky, "Send us Your angel band, to carry us away," she would chant, over and over, for hours at a time. For days, those were just about the only words she'd spoken, when she spoke at all.

After a few mornings, the sky cleared of the smoke of the invaders' fires, but poor Chellie's mind never did. She never was "right" after that and spoke words no one could ever make sense of.

Chellie was Pink's Aunt Chellie, his pa's younger sister, born on the place in 1845, and she had survived long enough to see dire hunger and famine and the loss of her world. She died at twenty-five with her prayer for the band of angels still on her lips. Meteors flashed in the dark sky that night as she breathed her last.

Mister Pink's father told him this tale. It was he who'd heard Chellie moan, and it was he who reburied the little girl, covering her up again with the scorched soil of this place. Chellie had died a decade before Mister Pink was born, so all he had of her was from handed-down tales. Still, it seemed he'd known her and she was yet alive, brooding there, waiting for him patiently at the edge of the trees. When the tallest pines would moan and sway during a great wind, Mister Pink knew it was with her voice. When the dark soil called out to him to come and rest, he knew it was sometimes with her words, other times with those of others gone before.

"No wonder the earth cries out to me," Mister Pink said to himself, as he put aside this story by the embers of his fieldstone hearth on which he often cooked his meagre meals.

The bricks of the fireplace kept their warmth, but

there in the shadows of the cavernous room sat Old Stephney, for Pink's people, the name of the personification of grief, want, and desire, of unsatisfied longing, of the drawn face of starvation and irreparable loss. There the old crone hooded in black waited for Pink and would not go away. Her shrivelled face with its sharp nose and shrunken mouth was always turned slightly away, so that he'd never be able to look in her eyes.

Still, she waited in the shadows, moving, swaying, like Aunt Chellie had done, as she moaned on the steps of her little house years before.

This time, the moaning was Mister Pink's, a low, scarcely audible, deep inside moan, as he sat by the ashes and finally wet them with tears.

"They's all gone now. My Goldie, and now me—ninety-three years old this year—I'm the very last to go, and all alone," he said to the shadows there. They moved uneasily. For Mister Pink, the shadows were all there was to listen, to talk to.

"Looks like my only true blood kin is sleep," he said at last.

And with that, he picked up his kerosene lamp that gave out a wisp of soot at its moving, and the old man made his slow way to his bed.

III

Of Rabbits and Hawks

~ ✿ ~

The new morning came with a freshly defiant light after the long limbo of dark. The ghosts departed sometime deep in the night, and Mister Pink finally slept as if he'd been given a numbing drug. No wakings, then finally not even dreams. Now on this new morning, he felt rested and at peace.

Part of Mister Pink's knowledge bred on the land was that cataclysm and loss were a part of the natural rhythm and not the end of the world, that nothing lasts forever, neither victory nor defeat, droughts nor floods, winter nor spring. If the hailstorm took out the entire corn crop, the cows still had milk and the chickens were laying, and he could grow a new crop of corn next year. No matter what dread thing would overtake them, the old could tell stories within the land's rich experience as stars by which to steer. In a parched season, the old would remember that in 1875 the great rivers dried to a trickle and even cows died. If the summer was cold, it was not as cold as the year they had frost on the first of June. If the winter turned mild, it was not as mild as when roses bloomed that year on Christmas day. The people had long memories and were very tough. They had been beaten so many times that they couldn't be frightened any more by any kind of hard prospect. They'd hung on so long now in spite of everything, they couldn't think of any sort of threat that would make them quit. And as for Mister Pink himself, his ancestors were just him in another age.

After so many years, this was the way his mind was bent. The planting of a seed or birthing of a calf was the start of a cycle that didn't end. As soon as the crop was harvested, or even before, hopes for the next planting began deep down. The truth that tilling the land had no ending—that was part of its wisdom sure, and Pink, for all his simpleness, had drunk deeply from that spring.

Just yesterday, Mister Pink had noticed that a slender green shoot had appeared at the base of an ancient oleander killed back last winter and that he'd thought dead. New life—it was the renewed evidence of the determination to live. Its modest green brought Pink comfort and encouragement too. The will to live had proved unconquerable, then, in spite of biting frost and some of the bitterest cold winds he'd known. At that moment, Pink had felt that his determination to struggle on was greater than he'd thought.

This was drama better than any stage, but he even found

comfort in the renewal of the most monotonous of nature's routines, cyclical and repeating endlessly as they were too.

After his breakfast was made and the plates washed, Pink looked from the door to see a figure walking in silhouette across the crest of the hill.

"Up with the whippoorwills," Pink smiled to himself.

In stark, angular relief, the figure was, the bright morning sun behind him, casting a long shadow before. The figure looked like a cardboard cutout—one-dimensional, as if pasted on a homespun white linen cloth. It turned into the lane and with its usual strong stride, came jauntily Pink's way. It walked into its shadow till the shadow was eaten up and gone, and all was golden with light.

Mister Pink had known the minute he'd seen the figure's powerful way of walking, that it was Triggerfoot Tinsley, a young friend who lived in the Tinsley family's old farmhouse tucked into its red-clay hill just over the ridge. Mister Pink had grown up knowing the Tinsleys and remembered the day Triggerfoot was born. There was great rejoicing over there because the baby was their solitary child, and born into the couple's old age, long after most folks had thought Mrs. Tinsley was past childbearing time.

Mister Pink recalled Trig's mother, Miss Ascenith, one of the kindest and gentlest ladies he'd ever known. Her death a decade ago was a great loss to all around. He remembered how Trig and his pa dealt with it the best they could.

Triggerfoot's father, Mister Will-Wallace, had died a few years back about the time Goldie had died. He was Trig's last close relative, so the son was now, like Mister Pink, pretty much alone in the world.

"Mister Trig," Pink hailed him, "you're out mighty early today."

The sound of a red-tailed hawk sent its plaintive cry through the still morning air. Out hunting, no doubt, for a rabbit to feed its young, housed high in their nest in the tall tulip poplar just into Mister Pink's woods.

A wren scolded at the house's eve.

Like the hawk, Trig was hunting too. He had with him his old rifle, which he called Swinge-cat. It was slung cracked open on his arm, and Towse his dog darted eagerly this way and that from his heels.

"The pantry needs rabbits," Triggerfoot replied. "And so do I. Don't imagine old Mister Pink would turn down a nice plate of young fried rabbit neither, I 'spec."

"And I 'spec you're right," Mister Pink smiled his assent, happy to see his lively young friend.

It did Pink a world of good to have the young around. The older he got, the more he craved their company. They stepped lively as his feet no longer could. For all the world, Mister Pink felt that his brogans had lead soles that weighted him down—like having anvils inside, he sometimes said to himself after a particularly hard day.

As usual, Triggerfoot, Swinge-cat, and Towse had been successful in their morning kill. It had taken but a few minutes' walk to bag all that he'd need. He could have had half a dozen more for a little extra time, but Triggerfoot hunted only the fresh meat for the day, and didn't kill for sport. The hunt was too much the fabric of his daily life to be deemed special recreation in the way city and town folks said. In the winter months, he didn't shoot rabbits at all. Six or eight rabbit boxes precluded the wasting of shot. That store-bought commodity, he reserved for wild turkey and deer. Triggerfoot about lived off of venison in the cold days of the year.

Today, his old leather pouch that he had slung round his neck looked like a belly after a big calabash meal. Its bounty testified to the skill both of Towse, who was counted one of the best rabbit dogs in these parts, and of Triggerfoot, whose aim was truly expert. Both he and his rifle were real swinge-cats at that, and so the rifle's name. As for Towse, several city folks had tried to buy her, but Triggerfoot would have none of that. No amount of money could accomplish the deal. As he said, "Towse ain't for sale." And that was that. No use to say more.

"Nailed this'un clean in the head, so they won't be any shot to break off one of them few toothies you got left," Triggerfoot said as he held up the lifeless rabbit by the hind legs and placed it on the edge of Mister Pink's porch.

The head on its limp neck dangled and looked surrendered. Its clenched mouth bespoke a final sharp agony. The fur in places was rumpled, showing its soft cotton white beneath its dark grey. The shot had passed cleanly through its brain and didn't even draw blood. The hole wasn't discernible. Its supine body looked like an old thrown-away rag.

The two men knew the drill. They'd kind of eased into the arrangement, if arrangement it could be called. The word was too formal a business term for what they had.

There were three rabbits in Triggerfoot's pouch, enough for the day.

Mister Pink unstiffened his legs and led his young friend around the side of the house, where there was an old post made from a cedar cut off of the place. Around it were nailed some heavy cords, hanging down like strings on some ancient village maypole. With these, they tied the hind legs of the rabbits securely to the post, then put a tack through each hind foot with an old hammer which Pink left there for the ritual that was enacted most every weekday.

Mister Pink's sharp butcher knife made the proper cuts, and with pliers and some hard pulling, they soon had the little creatures skinned. With this accomplished, the only fur left on them was at the feet where the cords and tacks held the rabbits secure.

Towse and Pink's old hound Bleat had also paid their morning greetings to each other. Not even sniffing, they were familiar enough to be at peace, quiet like old friends. Towse sat on her haunches and watched her master's every move. Bleat, sitting opposite, did the same.

The skinned rabbits looked like the coloured drawings of an anatomical chart. They were all just shiny dark red muscle that attached to their brittle bones like clotted strings.

"Mighty good eatin'," Mister Pink said. "That young rabbit yestiddy mornin' was prime good feed."

Triggerfoot knew the story of Mister Pink's loneliness, with his wife dead and his younguns all moved far away. He knew Mister Pink looked forward to their rabbit cleanings or any other excuse for him to come his way. And truth was, Triggerfoot did the same. The death of his father still made him brood.

The old seemed to be mostly forgotten in this rush-to-make-a-living world, but Triggerfoot's world didn't operate that way. It ran mostly to remembrance and the rhythm and tune of what he called "old-fashioned time." For one so young and physically hale and hearty as he, he was unusual that way.

To Trig, "old-fashioned" meant hunting with Towse, fishing in the great river with a cane pole, ploughing an arrow-straight row, sitting on Mister Pink's porch for a spell, or walking (not riding) several hours to town.

On such a trip, sometimes he'd slow his pace so Mister Pink could walk with him here and there. Triggerfoot would listen and learn from his gentle friend.

"Old man Jones put up a six-foot fence to keep the deer out of his peas," Trig might volunteer. "It didn't work a-tall. So he raised it up to eight foot. That didn't either. At nine he quit. They still got in."

"Not surprised," Mister Pink answered. "'Specially with pea vines. Pindars is another. I've seen some deer pull up the vines to eat the green pindars." By "pindars," the old man meant "peanuts." Both he and Trig called them that in the language of the place.

"Nine feet! How high you reckon deer would jump?" Trig asked his friend.

"High enough," was Mister Pink's succinct reply.

Passing by a farmer's okra patch, Mister Pink might pause. "That field needs a scarecrow to keep off the deer," he'd remark. "See how the okra leaves have been cropped away. Get good and sweaty wet and leave your shirt hanging on the scarecrow at end of the day, when you knock off work, and more likes as not you'll never see deer."

Trig had tried this remedy in his okra patch. After a long August day, he tied his wet shirt around the scarecrow's neck. The salt of his sweat had dried white in the sun on its sleeves, where it glittered like mica flecks in the sand of a mountain stream or the dunes of the shore. Then he'd made a belt of his perspiration-soaked denims, tying them by the pants legs round the scarecrow's waist. Last, with his shorts, he decorated the crown of the stick man's broken straw hat, whose band already sported a bronze feather of a wild turkey he'd found just this morn at his door.

His shoes and socks in hand, Trig walked across the fields toward home with his usual stride, unconcerned, showing no haste, and with no self-consciousness at all. For true, he lived so far out, there was no one to see. The breeze cooled the sweat that glistened on his chest, and he felt suddenly even freer than the usual.

As he strode, Trig looked straight before him. His thick curls shone in the August sun and moved with the wind.

He liked the free feel of the wind in his hair. It was freedom brought tangibly home to him; and from his history lessons in school, he understood the ancient custom that Roman slaves had to have their heads shaved and only free men could have locks like his. This was one of the bits of information that impressed him, and he'd remembered it to this day. On this fine labour-filled afternoon, his senses were honed to a sharp knife's keen point.

Glistening with sweat in the sun, Trig seemed to burn from within so that it might be imagined that if he did have on clothes, most surely they'd have been scorched away. Anyone who stumbled on the scene would have sworn he'd encountered some battle god or sun deity of old—perhaps shining Cuchulainn or even the gold-helmeted Lugh of earliest Celtic lore, for, indeed, these were Trig's cultural inheritance as certain as the Southern soil.

On this particular afternoon of the scarecrow decoration, Trig had been happier than the usual with his day's work, so he whistled a jig on his way. A gathering of noisy big blackbirds followed him, swirling around his naked frame.

Trig felt at one with the sun and breeze. It was as if he'd grown up straight out of the place like a gold-tasseled stalk of corn or a tall oak in full bronze leaf in the lambent morning light of fall. The corn moved rhythmically with the wind; the oak limbs swayed.

And in Trig's okra patch from that day forward, there were no more deer, so he listened alertly for such little bits of farming wisdom Mister Pink could offer his way. "Yes, offer," Trig said to himself, for such he knew to be gifts indeed.

When Trig congratulated his old friend on the success of his advice, giving the details, Mister Pink had the final say.

"Well, thanks for the praise, but have you stopped to think it might have been sight of you nekkid that did away with the deer?"

Trig had to smile at that. "You got a point," he answered his friend.

Triggerfoot liked the way Mister Pink merged the land with himself and himself with the land, when he'd talk, for Trig himself was wont to do so as well.

"Ain't had no rain on me since the first of June," Mister Pink would say. "I reckon I'm going to dry up and blow away. I'm as dry as tinder, and just a spark could bust me into flame." Or better, he might declare, "The grass is all over me. I got to get out that hoe or soon it'll cover my eyes, and I won't be able to see."

Lately, Trig had been telling Mister Pink that the seed corn was ripening on the special stalks set aside for producing the seed to be saved for planting next spring. Trig told his friend that he hoped soon to be about seeding a next year's family of his own. Mister Pink nodded his grizzled wool and agreed it was time. He'd picked up the signs of this before from odd bits of conversation with his friend. He'd gathered that the object of Trig's attention was one Becky Sue, a blue-eyed beauty in town.

No. Trig was not too young or obtuse to listen to Mister Pink. For all his liveliness and reputation for high spirits about Clay Bank, he had a thoughtful, sharp-minded side. For all his good humour, he was not a frivolous lad and thought of the future more often than folks figured he did. He'd already come to the conclusion that in order to learn, you went to the wise. And as Trig saw it, Mister Pink had ninety-three years of living stored up inside. You couldn't live that long without getting wise. Once he'd told Mister Pink, "It's sure better to ask a question and look a fool than to keep silent and stay one." His friend agreed, but in his wise way also cautioned him against idle talk, knowing, as he said, that no one has a finer command of the language than the person who knows when to keep his mouth shut. Trig told Becky Sue, who'd mentioned he ought to go to college or at least trade school, that he had his college at home, that if the eagle wanted to learn, he'd waste his time seeking out crows. That silenced her for a time.

Mister Pink and Trig were scrupulously honest with one another. They didn't even tell white lies.

On the subject of honesty, Triggerfoot once said to his friend: "It used to be that you could count on a man's word. A man said he'd stand by you, and he would. A man said he'd kill you, and you'd best move along. Workers worked, and on time. A man said he'd be at your place to help you do some work at noon, he'd be there five minutes before time. Nowadays, seems like you can only count on most men to beat you out of whatever they can, and tell you lies as easy as swatting a fly."

To this solemn reflection, Mister Pink gave a sad nod of his head.

Pink and Triggerfoot were both good with their hands. They had this in common too. They could turn an axe handle and put a helve in it, could use the plane and drawing knife with skill. Mister Pink could peel, strip, and cure his own white oak, and cane as pretty a chair as any woodworking master could. His split oak baskets, besides being serviceable and durable, were delights to the hand and eye. His cone-shaped fish baskets were much in demand in the neighbourhood. The two friends had this same knack with wood, in just about any way you could imagine—with hammer and nail and dowel and peg, with dovetail and chisel and gouge.

As makers fashioned in the image of the Creator of all, they had worked long at turning the jumbled rough wilderness of time into a habitable smooth garden. For them, it was not disobedience that was the lesson of the fall, but of chaos's return—the sorrows of knowing disorder, whose end is unalterably, death, in a cannibal world.

Their loss of innocence was no fall, but, instead, in its own way, a quickening to life, in which they'd tried to bring some measure of temporary order into the flux. They had entered the rhythm of being and had reckoned with the process of time.

Today as the two men were cutting up the rabbits and

salting them in turn, placing Mister Pink's in an old white ironstone bowl, and Triggerfoot's in a clean canvas bag, they talked about the crops, from pindars and field peas to watermelons and corn.

They'd both had pretty good luck with pindars this year. They'd helped each other with the tedious task of pulling up the plants, shaking loose the soil, and detaching them from the roots of the vines. A tiresome task it was; that is, if you had to do it alone. With the two men talking at ease, and enjoying the give and take of speech that had pauses like the refrains of old ballads punctuating the work, the time passed and the work got done, without in the least being a trying affair.

And then the two had them a good pindar boil in Mister Pink's big black iron pot outside under the trees. The salty taste of boiled peanuts always brought back memories of Mister Pink's childhood, and he'd talk long and long about the old days as he and Trig would sit on their cane-bottomed chairs tilted back against the porch wall and eat at ease, throwing the shells beyond the porch floor.

Mister Pink was true to his race in loving watermelons as a favourite food. Trig liked them too, but not as much as his friend. An African fruit whose seeds crossed the Atlantic in slave ships of old, it, like okra, and the people themselves, had taken good root and multiplied in the rich Southern soil. The sweetness of melon seemed to be a perfect match to the warm place itself.

It had always been hard for the black folks around here to resist watermelons. His pa had told Pink that back in slavery days, Old Maussuh Richards in desperation had to make plaster casts of his slaves' feet to serve in matching the footprints of culprits who were always raiding his prime watermelon fields. At the remembrance of this, Mister Pink would always laugh, because he figured he'd have been one of the thieves himself who'd have used desperate means to liberate a few. Yes, his feet no doubt would have been immortalised in plaster like theirs.

In this, Pink was in full sympathy with his forebears. He understood their desire and need. The stereotypical great broad smile joyously beaming over a watermelon slice was not a whit wrong when it came to him.

One of his daughters—Verta May, by name—who'd gotten up high and mighty in this world, had her a good job in D.C. Mister Pink could remember that about a decade ago, he was having a particularly good watermelon year. So with the help of Goldie, the daughter decided she'd take one home with her in a tote bag on the passenger train back to D.C.

Now, like her mamma, Verta May had a good sense of humour and could see the comic and ridiculous in the world around. Like her pa, she could see the humour in herself too when she was involved, and was continually ready to laugh at herself when deserved. That too was a farmer's way. Mister Pink could often be heard to say, "Well, that was shore dumb of me, plumb stupid," and laugh.

Well, it seems that on this rather highfalutin' AMTRAK Silver Meteor Miami-To-D.C. train, Verta May was seated in first class, among nothing but white folks, mainly from the Yankee resorts in Florida, she reckoned, from the way they talked and dressed and the urban values they expressed.

Verta May had some pride and figured that when she got on, a rural black woman at the AMTRAK station in Columbia, South Carolina, the passengers would infer some stereotypes of her accordingly. Leastways, that was in the back of her mind. So she did her best to act prim and proper and make certain to talk in the very best way she'd learned in D.C.

She was dressed in her finest fashionable summer travelling clothes and was pleasant and elegant in her graceful way. And Verta May was accounted a very handsome woman anyway. She had kept herself fit at an exercise salon. "No butt bigger than a number three washtub for me," she was sometimes heard to say. Though she laughed, she meant it too.

Seems she'd got all the railroad car quite convinced of her refinement, that is, till going through Virginia, the train had lurched and made a jolting stop, and out rolled her watermelon from its tapestried bag—spang down the aisle and bursting at the front of the car, the focal point of all of their views.

Its sweet carmine juice trickled in a rivulet past richly

shod feet, and its crunchy violet-red heart, all wasted and ruined, gave her double sorrow that liked to have drawn tears. There it sat on display, the heart of its sweetness violated by strangers' stares.

Verta May tried to look as if nothing had happened, but all the car judged at once that the watermelon was hers, as indeed it was true.

She said to her D.C. friends upon recounting the tale: "Try acting like a black woman who gets on the train in Columbia, South Carolina, doesn't have a thing to do with that watermelon. It would take an Oscar-winning performance to convince anyone of that," she had laughed to her friends.

AMTRAK was no Orient Express, it was true, but, yes, Verta May lived in a different world from Mister Pink and her ma, who had, as we've said, never left the county of their birth, never had the slightest desire or reason to, and weren't ashamed of what came naturally to them. And, as Triggerfoot thought of Mister Pink and Verta May, why should they? They say it's an African fruit, he reasoned. Looks like this new generation of African-Americans would play up the relation of continent to man, their heritage long from the old land to the new. There was this new thing called Kwanzaa and even bright-coloured African robes. Why wouldn't watermelons, okra, and sweet tater yams fit the same sort of scene?

But good reasoning seemed not to be a part of the day, as both Mister Pink and he knew. The world had become lopsided askew, all things tilted awry like that leaning tower in Italy Triggerfoot had once seen in his geography book at school.

Triggerfoot liked Verta May well enough the times he'd seen her on visits to her pa, 'cause at her pa's, she didn't carry around the burden of D.C. At home, she was just plain Pink's Verta May and would sit barefooted in her rocker and talk at ease. She always made sound good sense to him. And that readiness to laugh at herself when she did something foolish—Trig was like that too. Like with so many farm folks he knew, it was that sense of humour about themselves and their situation in the world that got them through.

Verta May was twenty years older than Triggerfoot, still single, and not likely ever to be otherwise. Men didn't interest her much at all. She'd made her career her babies and family too. Not that she didn't like children. Trig remembered one of her comments just last year. "What a sad world this would be without children," she'd said. "And what an inhuman one without the old." This was the kind of statement she was paid for in her announcing job in D.C., but it had impressed Trig as being wise and true. The irony that it was he, not she, who was getting the benefit of her pa's ninety-three years was not lost on Trig, dramatic TV pronouncements or no.

She was good at her job and well-liked up there. Her friends and associates liked Verta May. Now, in her mid-forties, she was at the top of her game. In a small circle, she was even something of a celebrity. Not that she acted the part. Instead of putting on airs in a show-biz way, she stayed plain. Instead of spending, she saved. She had simple ways by nature and had put away quite a sum of money, which she'd invested well.

Mister Pink always looked forward to her visits. She usually came in summer, not coincidentally, around watermelon time. Now for the past two years, she had come on his birthday, Thanksgiving, and Christmas too, promising her pa that this would become her routine. With her mamma's death and, at his age, she knew she'd be needing to take some care of him and be sure he was getting along all right. He wouldn't have a phone and was hard-pressed to write, so Verta May, except for these visits, was truly cut off from her pa.

Her brothers and sisters had even less time for him. They all had children, and some had grandchildren too, and were scattered from Houston to Detroit and Oregon. When they came home, Pink's children looked restless and ill at ease, as if anxious to leave the time they got there. Their own children looked around them as if they'd landed on Mars. Mister Pink had heard one of the Detroit younguns say of the place, "Man, what a hillbilly dump!"

They were all part of the television and movie and basketball-football set, so what could you expect? They lived in a fast-food McWorld, and were urban to the core, while old Mister Pink barely had electricity, certainly no basketball hoops or TV, and had never tasted a Big Mac or even heard of Disney World. The children at Mister Pink's, with the very world around them there, were mainly just bored. Pink felt that only the Houston lads might be redeemed. They took an interest in Mister Trig's hunts and liked to ask questions about how their grandpa did things on the farm.

As for the parents themselves, they were often glancing at their digital watches to measure the time they could leave. And that, Mister Pink could see out of the corner of his eyes, though he tried to let on he didn't.

So, to the young ones, Mister Pink was like some ancient time-stained monument in a big city square. You knew it was there on its heavy stone base, but you never stopped to read the brass plate to learn its name. If the figure got moved, you'd miss it, but only vaguely and never enough to inquire where it had been sent.

Their rabbit cleaning done, the sun was now beginning to be hot on the skin. Triggerfoot took his leave, and Mister Pink stayed behind.

That was the story of his life. Roads and railroads, even clay paths, they took people away and sometimes never brought them back. In the shadowed recesses of his mind, Pink feared the road, for the folks around here had ample reason to do so from their own people's past.

The road brought invaders who left them hungry and dug up the dead. The road took living children away and made them dead to home. It was as if the roads were veins that bled off lifeblood but never pumped it back in. For all of Mister Pink's life, the road had been mainly one way.

Now what had been the old community was hardly populated at all.

In the old days of his pa, the neighbourhood had been considered the distance in any direction from home that the family could comfortably travel by wagon or carriage, pay a visit, and return home in the same day. Today, with cars and paved highways, all that was gone. So were most of the farms.

The fine old family places, two centuries old, were left to grow up in weeds and the creeping in of pines. The old farmhouses were deserted and visited only by mould, rot, and decay. Tree farming was in; row-crop farming was out.

"Tree farming," Triggerfoot would say to his friend, "Ain't no farming at all. I'd rather raise sunflowers than trees." And Mister Pink had agreed.

Trig elaborated in his spirited way: "Cain't you just see me at Cousin Kildee Henderson's store though, and the men gathered around the pot-bellied stove. And I come in, and making the talk of the day, ask the crusty old crew, 'How's them sunflowers doing? Ralph, Spurgeon, Earl, how's your flowers bloomin' today?' Why even the fourteen-point buck head on the wall would have to laugh out loud."

At this, Mister Pink would only shake his head. At the incongruity of men raising flowers for crops, he could only smile.

"Well, then they might offer me a pink lemonade while they'd drink out of the jug, and hand me Kildee's missus' *Ladies Circle* or a fashion magazine. And I'd stop crossing my legs with ankle on top of knee."

As a matter of fact, though, sunflowers brought a pretty good price, especially the black oil kind. City folks were beginning to feed them to backyard birds in great elaborate miniature temples like mini Taj Mahals, and so sunflowers would have been a heap better venture than some others Triggerfoot's family had tried. Still, there was that thought of growing a crop of flowers for sale. As he thought of the very idea, in resistance to it, Triggerfoot crossed his legs ankle on top of knee.

"Adapt or die," was the harsh new motto of the times. And some, like Triggerfoot, would rather choose the latter than compromise or bend, for the many who chose the former still went under anyway. Triggerfoot's pa had said that the world's card deck seemed to be stacked against people like them, like all the aces and face cards were forbidden to come into their hands. That was the new game played in this new world. Those big men in power, in a far-off place, had invented the game, made up its rules, and dealt out the cards. For Triggerfoot and Mister Pink, the stakes were quite high. It had come down to this: they had to play but never expected to win, just struggled not to lose everything they owned. A fateful lottery this.

Triggerfoot was off on his way back home, with his pair of cleaned and cut-up rabbits in their bag in his leather pouch. The lone red-tail circled and cried its shrill hunting cry. It alone kept Mister Pink company now.

Although it was still early in the day, Pink thought he'd just sit awhile, and his head soon nodded for a few minutes' doze. For all the world, with his head down in sleep, he might've looked to a passerby like a rabbit crouched down and frozen motionless when the predator flew nigh.

IV

Resurrection Lilies

His doze lasted longer than the usual, and the sun slant-ing down on him was like a sundial telling time. Its rays now entered the porch and fell directly on his drooping head.

"One o'clock," Mister Pink said aloud, judging the time by the shadows from the slant of the sun and the objects it now struck on the porch.

"Well, this cottontail rabbit better be fixin' to hop on its way," Mister Pink said to himself. He'd had a pain in his arm and shoulder all day. "Must have been that hoeing I done yesterday," he said to himself.

Weeds and summer grass were growing in the paths of the sand-swept yard. The remnants of an ordered patterned garden were all about the house front running to the old carriage arc. In its prime, it no doubt had revealed an elab-orate, bright paisley design, outlined in boxwood.

Now only a single giant gardenia remained, standing over head tall off centre to one side. In the old days, there probably had been two, paired in balance, each to a side. For this was the nature of that world—order, balanced design.

The gardenia's blossoms, touched by the sun, now sent their fragrance around. Its rich glossy leaves were bright in the sun. The new startling white flowers contrasted with the ecru and yellow of yesterday's spent blooms, the very blossoms that last evening had glowed like white ghosts in the final quartering of moon. They bloomed their spendthrift day; and the next, were tattered, discoloured, drooping, ready to fall. The following morn, they would drop and be gone, but replaced by new rich white blooms. Fast to flower, fast to pass, but the evergreen leaves would stay. Through summer and winter, the foliage would shine in the sun.

It set Mister Pink to thinking, of things that would pass and things that would abide. To him, the flowers were like flesh, and the leaves that produced them, the spirit no man could define.

But today, what arrested Mister Pink's attention was the yearly phenomenon you could tell time by. Almost miraculously, overnight, in what were once the flower parterres among the paths, sprang up foot-tall green stems like spears. Their tips were a cluster of tight bright wine-purple buds. These each opened to be a radiation of eight lily trumpets with the mottled pink colour of dawn.

"Naked ladies," Goldie had called them. Mister Pink's mamma, from a more circumspect time, had said they were "resurrection lilies," as folks called them before.

Whatever their name, the lilies came up faithfully every year in late summer, and even though predictable as clockwork, they still always came to Pink as a surprise.

From no clump of foliage and out of stark dry and hard-packed bare ground, so rapidly rising, you'd have forgotten they were there. Yes, even now after nearly a century of seeing them, they still surprised him.

And joy, too, old Pink would say. Their bright burst of bloom on the bare stem had its proper message for him. Their colour was the very same tint of certain moments in the stippled sky of new day, or the inside of the conch shell from the far distant sea.

Today the air was so heavy with moisture and the fragrance of sun-touched gardenia that Mister Pink felt he could hold the air palpable in his hand, like some wonderful liquid, could scoop it up and bathe it all over him, like some fine ladies did lotions and perfumes and rare costly oils. The air was so thick and laden with fragrance that Pink found it a labour to breathe.

In truth, it was an air and a noon that did not invite work, but despite the heat and the pain in his arthritic hip and arm, Pink bestirred himself to pick up the giant heavy iron-headed flat hoe, forged in the blacksmithing days gone by, and chop out some of the grass clumps in the old garden paths.

The dirt paths of old would have been swept clean most every day with a handmade rake that would have left pretty patterns like sea waves. But now Mister Pink was lucky just to keep out the summer grass and weeds. He worked at this task just a little along as he had time.

Today, Pink felt even more worn out than his usual. But the resurrection lilies inspired him to action, and something about the heat and humidity betokened a much-needed late afternoon rain. The air was still, very still, like it was expectant, holding its breath. So today he was making good headway and had the paths successfully cleaned. Other than the shoulder, his joints seemed to work best in the heat of the day, like the heat was an oil that lubricated the metal of rusty old gears.

Swept yards kept away snakes, chiggers, ticks, and fleas. The yard chickens loved them for scratching up beetles and grubs. Mister Pink liked them too, for they brought back memories of Goldie and his mamma, Mamie Lou. It was a woman's sphere, but lacking women, he bent his back to the chore.

When Verta May came on her visits, she sometimes would pick up a hoe, but her tender manicured fingers soon got blistered from the rough handle of wood. They were accustomed only to pushing buttons and striking keys. The blisters would burst and then weep their tears. At that, Verta May would prop the hoe in the cool shade of one of the massive red brick chimneys that ran up each side of the house.

As she rested her shoulder against its solid form, the crumbling mortar from the pointing and the shaling of brick whispered to her of the passing of time.

It was a slow passage here; and today Mister Pink, lit by lilies, and alone in the promise of a fair summer's day, became a part of that passing. His heart finally gave out. There was a sharp pang, and he fell crumpled up to the ground. His last sight was the pastel colour of conch shell on the new opened lily blossoms his face had fallen among.

His last thoughts hurried to a fast blur of images—first to Verta May the previous summer propped at the chimney on her hoe, then to Verta May playing in these paths as a child with her brothers and sisters, Goldie hanging the new fresh wash on the line—then on back, to when he and Goldie were wed, further back to his pa and ma, first in their old age, then in their prime, to his own pleasures and pastimes as he grew up on this soil, then still further back to Aunt Chellie, to the days he had known only from hearing, of Berry Richards and old Master and Missus and their people on back before—then hurrying onward in blur of a string of sandhill cranes flying in long undulating pattern with the river as guide to a brimming, broad, dazzling sea.

It was about five o'clock before Triggerfoot found Pink. He was stopping by for a brief visit and chat to carry the simple news of the day. Little things of the harvest, or hunt, or the creatures he'd seen—these were mostly the extent of Triggerfoot's simple world. In that, as Trig had just been thinking today, he had something else in common with his friend. With the exception of Trig's senior class trip to Charleston, neither had travelled more than fifty miles from home, had ever eaten in a restaurant, ever wished anyone harm, told a lie on purpose, read or listened to much besides the Bible, or let a hungry dog go hungry for long. Their worlds were gentle and uncluttered with the great events of men and their enthusiasms and doings, so the two had time to live and be friends.

Triggerfoot knew right away there was no life left in

the body that lay face down in the yard. So without haste or hurry he lifted Mister Pink's shell and carried it inside to the pieced star quilt that covered the slumping mattress of Pink's old iron bed. As he had walked to the steps, the yard had the smell of boxwood mingled with the fragrance of gardenias and full-opened four-o'clocks, but the room was musty with Mister Pink's smell—its tall windows closed and the shutters all shut. Tattered rich tapestried curtains from a time long ago were at the sill. These had probably not been parted in years. All these Triggerfoot opened— windows, shutters, curtains, and all—to reveal in stark light of the declining sun, the sparseness and bare bones of the spartan life Pink had lived out there.

The brutal light allowed no illusions. Its starkness fell heavy on the scene. Not even the air breathed.

In Triggerfoot's arms, Mister Pink's shell of a body had felt light as a bird's. Now with all the life gone, it was like a bundle of dry kindling sticks. Both Triggerfoot and Mister Pink had gathered a many such fallen branches from the woods around to start up their big and long winter hearth fires. Now Mister Pink was like one of these bundles in his friend's arms.

Outside, the distant sound of thunder rumbled in the hills. Lightning brightened yellow for a second in the greying sky.

Mister Pink was correct. He'd rightly felt the heavy still air to be pregnant with much-needed rain.

V

The Watch

~◌~

In a gentle rain, Triggerfoot walked the two miles to the nearest phone with a heavy heart. At times tears ran down into a couple days' growth of copper-coloured beard. The tears mingled with the drops from the sky. But mainly his mind was set on getting Verta May on the line.

He knew where she worked, but not where she lived, and it was now after office hours. Her name was a godsend, rare as it was, only one Verta May Suber in D.C., and luckily she was not so big a celebrity as to have an unlisted phone.

"Miss Verta May. It's Triggerfoot, down in Maybinton here. Mister Pink died today. I don't think he suffered none."

The pause on the line was followed by what Triggerfoot could tell was the fighting back of tears. It was Old Stephney come back again, and Pink's old Aunt Chellie's swaying and moan. "What kinds of men dig up a chile and leave her for de hog to root?" was in between their words.

"It was his heart that just give out," the young man surmised.

Verta May told Triggerfoot she'd be at Dulles International within the hour, and asked if Triggerfoot would please sit by Mister Pink's bedside till she got there.

Triggerfoot assured her that of course he would. His long stride would soon get him back to Mister Pink's home.

He put down a five on the store counter to cover the call, but the owner refused it, overhearing, and knowing what it was for. Mr. Ed told Trig he was sorry about his loss. He knew how close friends they'd been since Trig's pa had died. Then Triggerfoot walked out into the stark light of loss.

The rain had stopped, and the sky had cleared. Steam was rising from the pavement. Even though it was close to setting, the sun blinded his eyes.

The young man was as good as his word. He went straight to Mister Pink's house door. He'd have done so anyway without the promise. Like Verta May, he hadn't wanted to leave Mister Pink alone. *Funny thing,* Trig thought, *she could leave him there by himself in life, but not in death,* but Trig soon put this out of his mind, as Mister Pink had done so himself.

By the time he got there, the shades of evening had come on. It was just past what the folks way back called early candle-lighting time, and the shadows seemed to move uneasily in the great dusty hall.

A few of Mister Pink's garments still hung across the hall on a crisscross tangle of lines. There was his old khaki work shirt, almost white and thin as silk from its washing and wear. The sweat stains that wouldn't come out showed under its arms. The frayed cuffs dangled tags of string. When Triggerfoot opened the front door, the clothes, set in motion by the air, almost convinced him Mister Pink was in them and moved.

"Mister Pink," he wanted to say, "what's for supper on the stove? I've got you a nice young rabbit, but it can wait till the morning to clean. I've got a story to tell . . . one you won't believe . . ."

Indeed, if he'd had a rabbit, cleaning would have to wait. Any story would have to wait too. Trig already knew that he'd miss telling Pink this and that, that he'd so want to be able to ask his advice and share his little triumphs and woes.

At this moment came the full realization that there would be no morning for his friend. The house seemed dead itself. What life had been in it, now was gone completely, all drained away.

Triggerfoot stopped still, struck by the silence and emptiness there. It halted his steps as if frozen entire.

He had often heard black folks' stories of the dead walking, their souls coming back at death to take leave of those things and places they'd have to part with, the things and places they'd loved and pleasured in most in life and wanting to fill themselves with as much of it as they could for the wait of eternity. It would have to last a very long time.

Of this returning, this hovering of dead round the living, he had no fear. He had experienced it with the death of his pa, and now would welcome his friend, if he were to come.

But the creaking of the floorboards had been only Triggerfoot's own. He paused, listening intently, and it was while he was standing still now in the dark hall that he heard the sound. It came from the dark bedroom where Mister Pink's body lay.

It first came as a low voice in a soft moan, then louder, breaking into a cracking, grief-stricken sound like a howl.

"Verta May?" he called out loud. But it couldn't be her. She'd not have had anywhere near enough time to get here.

And no. This was no human sound.

Those who knew Triggerfoot knew he'd do no backing down. He'd meet whatever spirit as would be there. He half hoped it would be Pink, Pink in some state or form.

Slowly and methodically, with a steady hand, he lit the kerosene lamp Mister Pink kept on the hall table by the bedroom door. Lamplight, candlelight the metaphorical admonition, the body of the world to remain mysterious and fearful, no bright searchlights to make it seem immediate and reducible to man's will, for still even beyond man's puny glare would lie the dark velvet of eternity, pricked only by the great light of day, the body so frail, the mystery so strong and irreducible. As Trig well knew of man, the foot must be nimble and quick, but it was never quick enough, and this the riddle, old when first posed, even older now, of the modest capacity of man, but the man who knew this, was more of a man, knowing he is both good and soiled by sin, with a soul to win or lose, and a soul lasting beyond the body's finitude.

"Pink?" he called.

Triggerfoot was conscious of the wick's fumes burning his nose. With taut body at attention, he entered Mister Pink's room.

The eerie wail resumed, this time piercing Trig's ears. No ghost, not of Pink or of anyone else. It was just old Bleat at the side of Mister Pink's bed. The flickering light from the kerosene lamp revealed him there, head out-stretched on outstretched paws, sounding his loss. His eyes were oblivious to Triggerfoot. Bleat made no sign that he'd entered the room. Triggerfoot rightly reckoned he was too lost in the singleness of grief to credit most any thing.

The kerosene lamp lit Pink's worn features. With the muscles relaxed, his face looked older and even more shrunken, like the images of mummies that had been res-urrected from tombs. His lips were so thin, they looked stretched over the teeth that remained.

The pattern on the bright pieced quilt on which Pink lay was the only colour and life in the room. It was no doubt of Goldie's own make, the work of her hands, maybe helped by her three daughters, probably even Verta May, and in that way, in the stitches and scraps of their worn-out clothing, they were all with him there, even Pink's father and mother too, whose scraps of cloth torn from their worn-out garments Pink might even have recognised in the starry design. No, even without Triggerfoot and Bleat, Pink wasn't alone.

Trig, honouring the privacy of Bleat's grief, said nothing and just let him lie. Tomorrow, he'd feed him, but now, like himself, he'd need no food.

He pulled up Mister Pink's blue chair to the side of the bed and sat down. He watched in the solemn spirit of the thing. From time to time, he ran his hand over his beard without feeling its roughness there.

At intervals, Bleat's whining would come; but just after midnight, it ended, and old Bleat slept. The kerosene lamp had burned out, leaving its smell in the musty, close air, and the three sat still in the silence and dark of the room.

Triggerfoot dozed in the chair till the waning three-quarter moon passed an opening in the heavy drapes and fell on his face.

This waked him to life and to the renewed realisation of the death on the quilt. The moon moving across the room soon fell on Mister Pink's face. Triggerfoot looked for a long time on his friend.

Somewhere outside in the dark, a rooster crowed, strangely, falsely, for the sun was yet on the other side of the world.

Again, the silence and still.

Then in the long shadows of the room across the hall, he could see her there, so plain and distinct, her sharp features outlined in the moonlight—Old Stephney, black-clad crone, seated with her hands propped on a skull-headed cane—Old Stephney, the dreaded, the inevitable spectre of hunger and loss. He'd heard Mister Pink speak often of her cowled figure; but he'd always thought it was just Pink's imagination, a fantasy from the rich mind of his friend and his people before. Goldie was always declaring that Pink often said more than he knew, and Trig figured that this was one such time. Now he knew Mister Pink wasn't making her up. Old Stephney was part of the place, and of Pink, and now him.

Yes, she was there as sure as he was. There was no mistaking her form. Bleat had seen her some time before Trig, as was the way of animals with haints. They would recognise them before mortals ever would. Bleat's ears pricked to attention and trembled. He raised his head for the first time since Triggerfoot had entered the room. Triggerfoot, following Bleat's lead, looked there too. And that's how Triggerfoot had first seen.

The dark figure made no sound. None of them did. It was like when the birds suddenly fall silent when the hawk flies overhead. The figure sat motionless except for the currents of air in her heavy sable robes.

The moon passed on across the sky, leaving the hall and both rooms in darkness again. Although he could no longer make out Old Stephney, he knew she was there, for he could sometimes hear the rock of her chair. Triggerfoot was at peace with her, and the quiet and dark. He'd made that peace in rehearsal of this night long time before. For one so young, he had some of the habits and understanding of the very old. No doubt being born an only child to a couple in their old age was a reason why.

Triggerfoot would miss Pink. Of that he was sure. He'd take care of Bleat, for his last remaining days. Towse, who'd been left out of all this in Triggerfoot's distraction and hurry to get to a phone, wouldn't mind. At least for a time, Towse and Bleat would largely make up Trig's world, a life, to Trig's mind, now greatly diminished and shrunken on its bare bones.

VI

Verta May

And Verta May was as good as her word too. She hastily
threw clothes and the things that she thought she'd need in
her biggest bag, got a taxi quickly to Dulles and was lucky
with flights. She efficiently worked the system, which she
knew well. A nonstop flight from D.C., to Columbia was
only three hours wait away.

These passed by with flashes of memory and thoughts of
the work she'd not be able to do at her desk, and of how to
get up funeral plans, and all she needed to do. While she
waited at the airport, she called her sister in Baltimore,
who was to get in touch with their brothers and other sister, scattered from Oregon to Texas.

At the Columbia Airport, she took the easy walk to a rent-
a-car desk, signed all the papers, and paid with her Visa Card.

She was thankful that the airport there was not crowded
with the usual maze of concourses and the hurrying of people
and long lines for everything. Thank the Lord she didn't have
to go through Douglas or Hartsfield.

She drove the fifty miles into the comforting familiar

black night of the country and reached Pink's home a little after sunrise.

In the violet light of the morning, she saw the grey house in black silhouette against the pale lime-green tints of new-risen sun.

She could make out that the front double doors stood open. The diamond panes of the transom and sidelights were lit from behind with the light coming into the hall from the east.

Bleat, recognising her tread on the porch, met her at the door. His sagging jowls and doleful brown eyes looked suited to the scene. She reached down and patted his head and smoothed the matted hair of his back with her manicured hand.

"Old Bleat . . . you were here," is all that she said.

Triggerfoot had finally fallen hard asleep. Verta May found him there on Pink's chair, quietly breathing in deep-chested rhythm, his head on his arm, like a bird sleeps head under wing.

It was hard for her to look at the lifeless form on the bed, but she did so without tears. Those, she had shed in private where no one could see, on the dark drive from Columbia. Letting herself go and with no one to hear in the night woods, she had done more than weep. She let her emotions free in a way she knew she couldn't have with all her close D.C. neighbours to hear. She startled herself with the animal sound of her grief.

Now she stood in silence at the foot of Mister Pink's bed for a good space of time.

Triggerfoot roused up from his sleep on his own, perhaps sensing that there was someone else from the land of the living now in the room.

He rubbed the sleep from his eyes and ran a hand through his thick shock of curls. The hand was large and square, lightly freckled and haired over with amber-coloured down. On his head, arms, and hands, his hair shone bright in the new morning sun.

"Verta May," he said. "I been here as you wanted me to."

"Thank you," she replied. "It's a comfort—you and old Bleat . . . to know . . . to know you were here."

But Triggerfoot would not tell her that Pink had died alone, and that he'd found him face down out in the yard some hours after his fall. Trig only hoped his friend had died instantly and had not lain there struggling and crying out in pain in the empty yard, but he couldn't be sure.

"I'll look for his suit," she said nervously, trying to find something to do, "and the new shirt and tie I bought for him two Christmases ago."

His suit was in the chifforobe where it always hung. It had the smell of dust and tobacco about it, and a faint smell of her pa himself. The shirt and tie she found in the bureau's top drawer, still in their unopened plastic and gift box next to all the little things he treasured most—a few yellowing snapshots of family, an old pocketknife with one of the blades broken off, and a nice new knife, a gift from one of the grandsons, a watch on a chain that had been his pa's, a gold cross on a chain that had been her mamma's and grandmamma's before.

Verta May knew he'd put the shirt and tie there, not because he didn't value them, but because he cared too much to use them—saving them for a future special day. It was a tangible symbol of her love he could touch and see. *A special day . . . well, now,* she thought, *that day is here.* He was always fixing to wear them. Now, in truth, he would.

She got these things together as Triggerfoot was taking his leave. He hadn't eaten in over eighteen hours, and Towse and the farm animals at home needed to be looked after and fed. There was a cow to be milked. Verta May would do the best she could there. She told Triggerfoot she'd called her sister at the airport, and she was to get in touch with the others for her.

Pink in off times on Verta May's visits had made it clear what he wanted his funeral to be. He wanted to be buried in a simple wood box in the graveyard there at the house by the side of his ma and pa. He would join Goldie there.

He didn't want Preacher Jones to make a long windy sermon over him. He wanted whatever words Jones had to say to be said in the house hall and be brief. He wanted his box to be carried on the shoulders of his grandsons to the grave. He wanted Triggerfoot to dig it and say whatever words there were said. And that was to be all.

Goldie, who had sung in the church choir, still had a good many friends there. Verta May was to tell them, and they would come, as they did for Goldie three years ago. He wanted only three hymns, and after all was over, he was to be marked, if at all, with the simplest of stones. Like for his pa, a fieldstone would do. As all the rest who were buried there, he would face east.

Most expressly, he was not to go to a funeral home. So before Triggerfoot left, Verta May sent him on the mission to find a wooden coffin, hard certainly to round up in these days of metal vaults; but find one he did later that morning on the top shelf of a back room at the old hardware store, that had been in business there in town for a century. He got the last one.

When the coating of dust was wiped clean, the wood was a polished rich walnut, a most beautiful job of dovetailed and beveled carpentry, most likely made by old Mister Hipp who'd died over two decades ago, shortly after Triggerfoot himself had been born.

The funeral would be the following day. Because it was summer and Pink insisted on not going to a funeral home, they couldn't wait the usual longer time of a local four or five days. In her organized, efficient way, Verta May soon had all this figured out and the funeral plans made. The simple service would be at three, and the choir and church ladies would serve a dinner at twelve on plank tables set up on sawbucks and covered with cloths under the oaks in Pink's yard. They insisted on "feeding the family," as they called it, a friendly old custom going back for as long as anyone could remember.

The walk to the cemetery would be a matter of minutes. No need to have hearses with their gears, noise, and fumes. No need for more. As Pink had wished, his teenage grandsons would carry the box.

With Triggerfoot's help, Verta May followed her father's directions to the letter as best she could. With the aid of Mangle Sanders, a relative of Goldie's, Trig dug a deep red-clay grave with pickaxe and spade. The gash in the verdant hill now told the tale. It was dry summer, and the clay was hard. Trig liked having all this to do. It set his mind on things he could at least halfway control, and kept him from feeling completely helpless.

Verta May dressed and laid her pa out by herself in his dark suit, new shirt and tie, and she and Triggerfoot lifted him gently to rest onto the white linen of the polished box. They left the lid open for the last respects to be paid. Her brothers and sisters would want to see their pa.

Verta May hadn't slept in two days now, so she got her some rest, back in the old bed of her childhood, where she had slept with her older sister till the sister married and moved away. Tonight, she wet the pillows with tears. Tomorrow would be another long day, but she had covered all the bases and done it the way her father had wanted her to. In that, she could rest easy in mind. Her brothers and sisters and their families would be coming in too, and since she was the one there, she'd try to make what home she could for them. She reckoned she'd have to take her mamma's place in making what welcome could be made. As for most of them, they'd probably prefer to stay in the Village Motel or Inn-on-the-Square in the town. The children, she knew, would all complain of no air. "It's hot!" she could already hear them whine. There, they could have air-conditioning and entertain themselves with TV.

VII

Rich

Richards Suber and his wife and son were the first to arrive. For short, folks called him "Rich," which at least moderately he was. He would joke and say he had a name to live up to after all. He didn't want to be like those supertall folks people called shorty, the big ones they called tiny, or the bald ones they called curly. But Pink and Goldie knew for whom he was named. Even though he'd been told, and it was a significant thing for them, it didn't much matter to him.

They had flown in to Charlotte on the first flight they could get from Eugene, Oregon, where he worked with Merrill Lynch as a broker and agent. The firm had trained him on a drive to get more minorities involved in the firm. Richards, who was bright and hard-working, was a good match in the scheme. He'd worked his way through the local branch campus of the state university while living at home with Goldie and Pink, and earned his degree in more ways than one. This looked sufficiently good on his job application forms.

He met his wife Marissa in Princeton, New Jersey, where he had been training at the brokerage school. She was from Newark and was taking classes at Princeton two nights a week. Rich, who was always conscious to "better himself," had met her at one of these. It was an unlikely match of country meets city, but somehow it worked, despite the cool, detached, and practical nature of both their personalities, or perhaps, as Marissa's mother had said, because of it. Above all, they agreed they wanted to succeed in this material American dream.

Their only child had been born five years into the marriage in Eugene. Both parents had careers, and the five-year span was a convenient resting place to pause, that coupled with the advancement of Richards' salary, and the purchase of a respectable split-level home in a neighbourhood touted by the developers as "gated" and "upscale."

They named the baby Eugene, after the place they happened then to live—Eugene Suber, the newest of Mister Pink's line. They had mailed Pink and Goldie photos at his birth, then first birthday, his first birthday party (Eugene looking wide-eyed in the standard paper birthday hat beneath streamers and many-coloured balloons). Later came Polaroids of his first day of kindergarten, and his graduation from sixth grade. On their yearly Christmas visits, Goldie swore Eugene looked a whole lot like Pink, more and more each year. Others of the family humoured her in this, for, in truth, he did not, nor in any way acted like him. It was plain to Verta May and to Pink himself that he took more after Marissa and was developing her Newark ways. As for accent, he had the bland, lifeless accent of TV.

Not that Eugene was a bad child. He was good in school, in fact excelled, but he was dreamy, and his feelings were very easily hurt, at which times he would retreat into himself and a book and not come out for days—that is, if he could make up an excuse for staying home from school. At school, he'd scored very high on aptitude tests and shown talent at drawing and painting, and was classed as a gifted child. He was painfully shy, and his grandfather and grandmother were near total strangers to him. All this would likely have changed if he'd been there for more than three days out of the year.

Marisssa and Rich had found a counseller for him through his teachers at school, and his sessions, they'd thought, were doing him good. Best that could be said, though, is that all they'd done hadn't caused him great harm. The medications the doctors had prescribed nearly did, but Eugene's parents were smart enough to get him quickly off these.

Now at age twelve, Eugene's voice was not quite ready to change, but he was already squarely in that awkward, gangly stage. His limbs were stretched out, and he didn't know exactly what to do with them. Painfully self-conscious, he felt very much that he'd like to hide them and retreat into some overlooked dark place. He didn't like sports, or any such games, and hardly ever went outside in Eugene. He had no pets and didn't want one.

There he stood at six o'clock that morning behind Rich

and Marissa on the doorsteps of Pink's old porch. His father was calling out "Verta May, Verta May," as his mother shifted her weight from shoe to shoe. She'd always been nervous and a little uneasy on first getting there. Rich himself was little better. Their infrequent visits home to his dad had always been short. So there the three stood with three leather cases resting on the steps, the size of each case in direct proportion to the size of the person whose clothes it contained. Theirs was the tidy neat life that put everything in its proper place. The cases sat unevenly on the warped boards.

Bleat was the first to meet them at the door. He barked and growled, but at last made his peace. Perhaps he was remembering them from last Christmas. Verta May quieted him with a soft word and the touch of her hand.

Regal, she looked, in a purple plush bathrobe and her raven hair turbaned in a linen headcloth of white. She held her robe shut against the morning breeze with a clenched hand. The taut knuckles showed.

The old heavy doors slammed behind them, and Rich moved to the open coffin that sat in the violet rays of dawn just lighting the hall.

There lay his father, looking quite natural, at peace, it seemed, but for the Sunday suit, white shirt, and new silk tie. Otherwise, he was much as they'd left him seven months before.

Eugene was watching it all from behind, taking it all in with his as usual careful, attentive eyes.

No eye was wet. They were red, not from tears but from

no sleep on the long cross-country flight, which in itself was surprisingly absent of the usual snafus and tie-ups and delays that went with the game.

Still, despite some fitful sleep on the plane, they were tired, and after brief greetings, they all put down their bags and found a pallet or bed.

Verta May herself lay back down, and the house resumed its quiet less than thirty minutes after Rich, Marissa, and Eugene had walked through the door.

Verta May lay there thinking for a long time about her brother, and her own life. Rich had always wanted to succeed, and in his mind had done so. He was at the top of his game, but last Christmas he had confided to her that he'd gotten increasingly more restless in his job. He'd thought having more leisure time off was the key, but this hadn't worked out. He even admitted that his mamma and pa had enjoyed their whole day, every day, such enjoyment as it was, and didn't feel that separation between work and play that he felt. They'd not sacrificed a part of their day to enjoy the other part, not worked certain hours soullessly in order to achieve certain other hours for something they enjoyed. Rich and Marissa had even taken out time from their busy lives to attend a job-sponsored seminar titled "Leisure to Develop the Soul." The firm was correct in knowing that soulless working made bad workers and unhappy employees, and footed the bill for the seminar. They even paid for a class in opera. Rich was just beginning to have the faintest inkling that Pink and Goldie developed their souls in both their work and play. There wasn't this restless and unhappy divide. As for Verta May, she'd already come to that conclusion many years before.

Rich had thrown himself even more fully into his work while trying to develop cultural interests outside. Unlike Verta May, who acknowledged the divide, Rich didn't want to think about any of this. It was counterproductive, he knew. At the office, his boss called him Mr. Positive and predicted a great career for him.

Now Verta May lay in bed pondering how her life had become affected too much in this way. *Leisure to develop the soul,* she thought, *the treacherous fallacy at the base of her intellectual friends' lives.* Maybe that would be a good topic for the program spots she wrote for TV, if she could sneak it by her boss, who probably wouldn't approve.

"Leisure," such a beautiful word on the tongue, a sort of glorified full bank account in time. She saw Rich and Marissa striving hard to live, with their mamma and pa living effortlessly. She wondered if it wasn't because they were rich in things too dear to buy.

Then she had the vision of her world in D.C., of the pathetic paradox of the strenuous pursuers of happiness, of people trying to buy leisure time. *Such ones go so violently about it,* she thought, *with their golf and their cruises, their safaris to Africa, their ski weekends to Aspen, their game packages for Super Bowl weekends, their winter excursions to resorts in the sun—so frantically seeking leisure that they'd be likely to die of exhaustion before discovering that such a commodity is not purchasable with money at all.*

"Poor in time," she mumbled out loud to the dark. "They've got to spend so much of it in the machinery of living: subways, traffic jams, the parking garage, airports, shopping, dentists, doctors, psychiatrists, appointments, tax forms, checks to be written incessantly, and on and on. All these things so waste it, there's little time left to live. No time left to remember anything."

She also saw how at the opposite end of the spectrum from those who sought leisure to develop the soul were those who never dreamed of anything beyond the animal. They were little better than beasts, lost in the glands, driven into pasture and field. They even conceived of themselves as beasts. She encountered plenty of them in D.C., whether in the materially wealthy or the desperately poor. Having money or not had little to do with it. Yes, without anything worthwhile to lift you up, you became beasts of the field.

Were she around, Mister Pink would have reminded his daughter that the high and mighty, proud in their power, intellect, and position, making themselves gods of the world, were like that Babylonian king of old—who fell to the state of the beast and, on all fours, ate grass in the woods, and grew fingernails like bird claws. He was the mighty tree of his vision, as the prophet had foretold, cut down and with the stump tied and bound, and no way to untie the bindings to send out a new life's green shoot until he lifted up his eyes, and his understanding returned.

Verta May had come to conclude that it was only natural for those who think of themselves as beasts to first act like beasts, and finally then to allow themselves to be treat-ed like beasts. This seemed to her to be a kind of three-step evolution in reverse.

Yes, in the city, this was the usual awful divide. She lay in the dark imagining the two extremes—the beasts roaming the concrete or motoring the maze of asphalt, with those others in high windows protected, ethereal, smugly superior, intellectually aloof, gazing down—incessantly down—imagining themselves the managerial elite, the ringmasters of the show, a charade becoming increasingly more vulgar under the great circus sideshow tent of their world.

As she drowsed on the verge of sleep, she was disturbed to see herself behind one of those high windows. The face was half obscured by a half-opened white metal blind; but, yes, there was no mistaking, it was her own face, and the window was her office's own. She could even see her well-chosen junk cluttering its office furniture and walls. Its view of the Capitol's white iron dome seen through the traffic fumes was exactly that which she encountered each passing work day, each digital tick of the clock.

Like the discomfitting grit in the bivalve, the vision of her face there at the high window, superimposed upon that hazy dome, kept her from sleep. What pearl lining would she be able to secrete to allay that nagging bit of sand? This was the problem that had ever more often now come to her of late at the most unexpected times, visiting her with a vengeance, a dark nagging at the core.

At last the images faded, the face at the window drew a black velvet curtain, and she slept.

VIII

Eugene

~◦~

It was about nine o'clock when Verta May stirred. She looked through the dusty panes of her window to see the thick shock of curls at the old rabbit post. It was Triggerfoot, using his pliers to finish the cleaning of five young rabbits, to be fried up for breakfast for the people inside. He knew there'd be company that would have to be fed. No restaurant or even place to get a cup of coffee was close by.

The day was clear with an unusually bright sky of blue. *A good day for a funeral,* he thought. On such a morning as this, Mister Pink always said the sky smiled. At that remembrance, Triggerfoot himself smiled. He saw Verta May at the window, and to her, he nodded "Good day."

Eugene had come quietly to the corner of the house and watched Triggerfoot for awhile. He was both repulsed and fascinated with the work of Triggerfoot's hands, now fully covered with blood. He stood very much like Bleat and Towse, silently watching the scene, his artist's eyes picking out details: the wet matting of fur, the drops of dark blood on the skin of Triggerfoot's hands.

Triggerfoot was deft at his work, a master for having performed this task hundreds of times since about Eugene's own age. He'd helped his father, and when his father went down with the cancer, he'd taken over the job—at about age sixteen.

In the last year, before his father succumbed, when they'd caught rabbits in boxes, and they had to be killed with a sharp blow to the head, his father had gotten where he couldn't do it anymore, so it had fallen to Trig. Now Trig thought back on this, of the gentling nature of his pa as he himself approached death.

Today Trig was thinking of this as he wiped himself up with his old navy blue bandana, blotting the blood that had spattered on the hair of his powerful right forearm.

Eugene's life was about as far removed from Triggerfoot's as was possible, or so it seemed. His schooling was to screens, watercolours, the pages of books, desks, the insides of rooms, the pavements of men.

Triggerfoot was conscious of him there, but when Eugene became conscious of his consciousness, he backed away and returned to the shadows inside. Still backing so, when in the hall, he bumped into the corner of Pink's coffin, which caused it to jar. The sharp edge of the coffin smarted as it caught his side.

At this, he sought out the quiet of a dark corner and a worn overstuffed chair. Its musty smell caused all his allergies to burn. He was already on medication for asthma, even at his young age, and the riot of pollens and dusts in this exotic place was playing havoc with him. His mamma had gotten rid of the cats that she'd desultorily owned, and the animals here with free range of these rooms played their part in this latest attack. He carried his medicine and inhaler in his pants pocket, but was so numbed with the strange day, that he hadn't thought to use them. He struggled to breathe.

There was too much to credit. He'd not seen death before. The skinned helpless rabbits that hung down from their cords, and the lifeless shrivelled up man there in the dark box, they all jostled his brain, very much as he'd jostled his grandpa on his linen when he bumped backwards into him.

Triggerfoot met Verta May at the back door. She was carrying her grandmother's old feather-edged ironstone platter in both hands. It had belonged to the Richards family a century before, when there was money for such serviceable English china that came as ballast to Charleston on the rich cotton ships that gathered the produce of a fruitful land.

The rabbits filled up the platter, their dark mahogany red making a rich still life against the crackled glass surface of white, and the feather-edged decoration of regal blue.

Verta May thanked Triggerfoot, and as he melted into the glare of the bright day, she carried the neatly cut up carcasses to the kitchen, where she soaked them in fresh milk, salted and floured and fried them in her mamma's great black iron skillet. A boiling pot of rice complemented the scene. They all counted on rice. For them in distant lands, it was the food that spoke most of home. A pot of rice on the stove, or even cold rice in the school lunchbox, let them know all was right with the world.

She'd made biscuits too, the way her mamma had taught her, and cream gravy as well. She fried up some of Mister Pink's famous smokehouse ham and made red-eye gravy to go with the grits. She found a jar of scuppernong jelly that her mamma had put up the autumn before she died. Its amber bright contents caught the light of the sun and reminded her of the gilding on the backgrounds of certain Renaissance Christ Childs and Madonnas she'd seen in the galleries of D.C.

Her mamma made the best scuppernong jelly in the world. Verta May had often thought that if Goldie could produce good quantities of it, she'd be a rich woman, knowing what price a D.C. specialty shop could get for a jar. Once having tasted it, a customer would pay anything to have more. "You could name your price," she'd told her mamma. Goldie, a little bewildered, as Verta May remembered now, had just smiled, but didn't say anything. Later, she told Verta May that Pink and the chaps were the only customers she needed or had time to feed.

At the breakfast preparations, Verta May was watched closely by Eugene, who, when invited to join her, sat silently at the old handmade pine table where the Subers had taken their meals for no telling how many years. It was polished smooth with use, and Verta May knew most every burn ring and scar thereon.

Verta May was about finishing her frying, when she was joined by Marissa. Marissa got out the plates.

"Seeing that pot of rice sure does me good," Verta May said to herself as she tidied up the stove with her dishrag.

Eugene laid forks and spoons. Mister Pink didn't drink coffee, so on her last visit Verta May had supplied the cupboard with her favourite ground roast from her deli in town. The shiny brown foil bags sat untouched, just as she'd left them at Christmas, their manufactured sheen looking oddly out of place on these shelves.

The coffee was steeping in a pot when her oldest brother arrived at the door.

This time, there were tearful greetings all around. Rich greeted and ushered him in.

The eldest brother, Berry, had flown in from Detroit. His wife and he were getting divorced and so she did not come with him. It was obvious to Verta May that he had his own cross to bear, and the last seven months had been hard on him. He had that look in his eye. It was going to be a messy split. Already, there were lawyers fighting over the house and children too. Later, Verta May would have chance to find out more from him, and offer to help if she could. His face showed the wear, and since she'd last seen him, his salt-and-pepper hair had turned totally grey.

Berry had two of his five children with him, two teenage boys. They were in high school, and since school was out, they'd not had anything else much to do. And he didn't want to leave them alone in the house. He never knew what these two would get into. Wife Sandra had refused to have more to do with them, or they with her, more accurately. Even with the children, the scene had turned ugly and was like to get worse. It was best to keep them apart. All this bore down on Berry with a tremendous weight. And Verta May bore some of it too.

The other three children, a son and both daughters, had sided with Sandra. The two eldest of these were out on their own now, and the youngest daughter, still in school, lived with her mother in an apartment building where she'd moved to be closer to her job.

Unlike Richards, both Berry and Sandra had blue-collar jobs and scraped by year to year. He worked on an assembly line and she in the cafeteria of the same plant. The children demanded all the costly things their peers had, and had been no help at all. So Berry and Sandra sometimes had to work overtime to meet the family's needs. He wasn't often very much at home. They never sat down together at meals. In fact, there were seldom meals. It was catch-as-catch-can, done rapidly, on the run. There was no semblance of a stable routine. Both Berry and Sandra slept when they could. They fitted their lives around their work routines. As the song goes, it was usually sleeping single in their double bed.

The whole situation put a strain on the marriage and finally had led to the split where they now stood. The pressures had simply been too much.

Through all this turmoil, as the news drifted to him, Mister Pink had stayed silent and didn't even shake his head. The first thing he would say, if he'd have been asked, was that Berry and Sandra needed to cut back on things. He would also have reined in their children's desires. Pink was glad Goldie had passed on before she had to witness the worst of their wrangles, especially since their eldest was her heart's very delight. As she'd once declared, she had to admit that she had a favourite but she wasn't saying who. It was clear to Pink, however, that the child was Berry, and had always been.

When he went away to take up this job, it had liked to kill her, but there wasn't any future there on a one-horse farm you didn't even own. So by circuitous route, first through a stint in the U.S. Army, then meeting with army friends, who enticed him away, or as he'd say, who'd given him his break, he had gone to work in this job. Though she never said so, Goldie regretted these friends' influence, but reckoned this just had to be.

The physical break proved to be another kind of break as well—perhaps several other kinds of breaks, now leading to a break in their marriage and all manner of internal fractures within the bonds of the seven of them. And this was in addition to Berry's own breaking of bonds with his mamma and pa, and where he was born. He was so cut loose he didn't rightly know who he was any more, or so he'd said to his mamma the last conversation they'd had. That night Goldie had cried on her pillow and asked the good Lord, the Good Shepherd of all, to bring His lost sheep home.

Since his mamma's death, to Berry the world had gotten

even more confused. No wonder he looked so thrown away.

The two sons Berry brought with him were a few years senior to Eugene, and of course thus deemed their cousin a child. When not ignoring him complete, they made sarcastic remarks, little jabs about his clothing and shoes, about his four eyes. He was a soft, easy target and didn't provide them much of a challenge, so got by relatively unscathed. They made it clear that he was beneath their contempt.

Eugene mainly stayed out of their way. He was taking to his Aunt Verta May, who, not having children, needed the attention of a surrogate child, and did special little things to be friends. She noticed how Eugene loved the way she poked a hole with her finger in one of the hot biscuits to fill it up with cane syrup, and she soon saw it was his favourite food. So she made him an extra couple and put them in the warming oven of the big wood stove. Just about mid-morning when he was alone, as he often was, she gave one of them to him, without a word.

Eugene recognised her sweetness, as sweet as the cane syrup he loved, and he'd have been made a conquest outright, if his visit could have lasted more than these few days.

There were three first cousins in the house now, and, despite their blood, it was as if they came from different countries of the globe. They regarded one another with blinking eyes like blind men seeing the first time in the bright light of a new day with the scales on their eyes just removed.

IX

Vermelle

~⟋∾⟍~

About an hour later, another of the Suber children stood at the door. Mister Pink's second child, Verta May's eldest sister, with whom she'd slept in the same bed till the sister had married more than two decades ago, was just her old plain unconcerned self. She hadn't changed a bit since she was a girl. The family joked that she still moved around so slowly that molasses in winter would be deemed fast in comparison to her. She talked as slow as she moved.

She came without her husband, Dawkins ("Dawk") Thomas, who was having to struggle to keep his job. She brought three of their five children with her. The eldest, Dawk Jr., was in service and was stationed at an army base near Heidelberg. The next son, Suber, was on a submarine somewhere in the Pacific, or, at least, she thought. She could never keep up with him. The two sons and daughter who accompanied her there were still in high school, about the age of Berry's two sons.

The Thomases lived in the big city of Houston, where

their father did menial work at the Space Center's mission control. They called Dawk a grounds technician, but in truth, 'round Mister Pink's country, they'd just call him a janitor. Leastways, he pushed a broom and made sure that certain doors were locked or open as the hour and situation called. He sometimes doubled as a kind of security guard, but carried no gun, and wore no badge.

The boys came inside Pink's old house, taking off big summer Texas ten-gallon hats. They said yessir and ma'am, and took right away to "Aunt Verta May." If it had been possible, they'd have liked to go fishing with Pink every day of the year, but a week in the summer and Christmas was all they could declare. They looked at their grandpa with a true sense of loss and what grief a fourteen- and fifteen-year-old could muster or spare, or let show.

Mister Pink's daughter's name was Vermicelli—funny thing about that. During her pregnancy, Goldie had for some reason craved Italian food, introduced to her palate by the owners for whom they tenanted the land.

They brought her several packages of Creamette brand Vermicelli to cook on her stove, in exchange for three foot tubs of bright red tomatoes she'd grown in her own special forty-foot row.

Goldie liked the musical sound of the word, so Vermicelli the child was named, though they soon shortened it to Vermelle. At times, when he was at his tenderest, Mister Pink called her Chellie in salute to that ancestor out of the old days.

Vermelle would not for a long time look at the figure in the wooden box. She walked near but would avert her gaze. It was as if her neck was frozen to iron, locked looking away.

When she saw Verta May standing quietly alone gazing down at her pa, Vermelle joined her, and the younger sister drew her in, putting an arm around her there, enfolding her in the bonds of shared blood and grief.

Vermelle looked at her sister's tear-moistened face; and she followed the gaze of Verta May's eyes to their object, and in this way she too was led to look at their pa.

It wasn't horrible. The dread of the sight was far more awful than the thing. There was her pa looking like she'd left him seven months before.

After a few quiet minutes, Verta May left her alone. She could weep then silently for awhile, but finally her grief reached crescendo in a sharp painful wail.

The wail stopped all the house. Even the dust motes in the sunlight seemed to freeze. Berry, who was lingering over his breakfast, stopped still, his mouth open, looking slack-jawed ridiculous, as a half-chewed mouthful of biscuit looked like plaster or school glue.

His children even looked up interested from the silly business they'd been engaged in on the floor.

Vermelle's children knew the sound was their mamma's. They'd heard it before, when their little five-year-old sister Florence had died from a fall at the playground at what seemed just a few years ago. It had near about killed Vermelle. Since then, she'd been more emotional than ever, and could not stand the strain. The boys, hearing their mamma, came to her aid, wrapping long arms around her there.

As Verta May often said, Vermelle lived in a perfect sweet world of her very own make. When the real one that was not so perfect crept in, there was pushing and shoving that left her wrecked on the shore.

The wail seemed to last beyond time. It held absolute sway, curvetting and pirouetting about the rooms like some dancer in the enthrallment and magic of complex arabesque. As it sought out all the shadowy, out-of-the way places on its way, it wavered and settled in the dim corners of rooms, in the secret spaces of closets and cupboards, saturating the dark beneath the floorboards and into the pitch black of the garret air.

The wail extended beyond the rooms to Mister Pink's yard beyond. It moved rustling through the great dark gardenia with its yellowing blooms. It startled a rack-heavy buck that had wandered groggily out of its lair. It fell gently on songbirds that stopped singing in mid-note.

Its echo paused as it ran past the graveyard where lay buried Goldie, Grandpa Suber, Berry Richards, his ma, pa, and kin. There it circled their stones and a part of it settled on the pit of the new dug red clay. Next it found its way cross the crest of the hill to the east where it caused a giant bobcat to stop in mid-stride, a paw held up frozen in midair, its fuzzy pointed ears at attention, alert—then fell with the drop of the land down Mister Pink's lush corn rows in the bottomland. It finally came to rest as it settled in the mists of the deep grey river's ripples and waves.

Then Vermelle was through. Her last wail broke off with exhaustion and too much grief to go on, and found its way to the shrouded figure of Old Stephney who sat unrecognised in the dark chimney corner, unseen by all but gentle Verta May. She wore her head cowled so her face in the shadows could not be discerned. Stephney knew the sound very well, as akin to herself, one of her own closest blood. She slowly nodded her head at Verta May in recognition and greeting both. Then silence, and now in the old house for quite a long spell, dead silence continued to reign. It was as if the echo of Vermelle's wail of grief had soaked up, exhausted all sound, had drained the colour from all things, had, in fact, used up the world.

X

Mamie

~·∾·~

That silence was broken by the arrival of the last of Mister Pink's children. It was late morning now, with the sun approaching its zenith overhead, when Mamie—Pink and Goldie's youngest—drove into the front yard. She was named after her grandmother Mamie Lou, and sometimes Mister Pink had called her by her full name.

As is often the case, the "baby" of the children had for her mamma and pa a special place in the circle of home. They'd not been able to give her any of the things of the world when she came along. Not that any of the children had had much, but she'd had even less. The times had grown harder. It cost more to live. Farm produce brought less, and everything else cost more, at a time when a child at school saw others have more and more. Mister Pink and Goldie made up for this in the little ways they could.

By the time of their last three children, the schools had become consolidated, and a yellow bus met them about a mile away where their dirt road met pavement. There, after their walk from home, Mamie Lou, Verta May, and Richards would stand with their satchels and lunch pails rain or shine. Pink had knocked together a little flimsy shelter for them with scraps of wood and a piece of rusted tin that had blown off an old barn.

Because Pink was handy with wood, the shed was a proper country copy of a city bus stop. He'd built in wooden benches for when the children had to wait long, which often they did.

Mamie Lou was the studious one. She'd use that time to read, her book spread open on her knee and smoothed by the palm of a hand. What with the struggle to make ends meet, the chaps had to help out with chores when they got in from school. So both Pink and Goldie would do a little more to ease her share. It was Mamie who always couldn't wait each year to get her new textbooks to look them through, sometimes reading the whole of them in the first week. Now it was fitting that she was working in the venerable Enoch Pratt Library as a librarian in old Baltimore.

Once, before she'd learned her *ABC*s, she took one of Verta May's grade school books to her pa to read. He looked at the pictures and read for her tales of wonderment. But strange, when Verta May or Vermelle read these same pages to her, they were different and very tame. It was only later she learned that Pink could not read, and was inventing the stories himself. This gave her a respect for books and the written word, but she missed the story's moral in forgetting how much better her pa's stories had been, coming out of the living rich details and specifics of time and place. Now it was books that figured centrally in her life.

She was still the baby to Verta May. It was her older sister, living nearby in D.C., who had helped get her the job. They kept in the closest touch of any of the siblings, being geographically the closest, as well as the sisters nearest in age and sensibility.

Verta May met her and her daughter little Goldie at the door. Her husband Byrd was travelling in Canada on business and would not be able to get there on time. Her other daughter Dinah, who had married at the tender age of sixteen, was expecting any day now, and in fact was a few days past delivery time. She wouldn't hazard the trip. Mamie had to tie up things at the library, short-staffed as they were this week with summer vacations and all, before she could pack the car and get on their way. She was lucky she'd been able to get there at all.

So Mamie and little Goldie stood there silent at the door. For Mamie, walking over that threshold with her pa dead was to cross some sort of Rubicon, a kind of River Styx. It was her Lethe and Jordan combined. Her feet paused at the threshold that had been worn paper thin by her own feet and those of her kin. She knew that when she stepped over, her own youth would be gone.

For all of the children, they realised that now neither father nor mother stood as a shield between them and death. They'd now become the shields for their children in turn. But as for themselves, they were orphans now, without protection by parents' hands.

Yes, Mamie Lou was the most serious one of Mister Pink's chaps. She was a bit more the sheltered, the more retiring, the quietest of the brood. Little Goldie was not much like her in that. She was a bundle of energy, bouncing about, asking questions about everything. It was all Mamie could do to keep her contained. Doing so, or at least trying, sometimes near about wore Mamie out.

The two stood at the door in dark silhouette against the bright sun-scorched yard, the tall spare figure like a statue holding the hand of an eight-year-old bundle of spirited doing. Mamie stood in place and shifted her weight from foot to foot, suitcases in hand, waiting for someone to open the screen door.

Verta May drew them in with no word. Mamie had wiped away tears, and Goldie was calming down. Past Verta May's shoulder, Mamie could see the box where her father lay. She went straight there to look on his face. She viewed him in silence, Goldie in hand.

The two sisters had a few minutes to themselves before they went in to the parlour where Berry sat with his bored-to-death lads. Their greetings were broken off by the arrival of the church ladies who were just bringing in the dinner and needed some directions from someone on where to set out tables in the yard for the food.

The sawbucks were soon laid and the wide hand-planed poplar boards placed upon them. These were the tables they used for such communal occasions as their Big Meetings, reunions, and dinner on the grounds. The six printed tablecloths brought by the various women, were each a different bright colour and design and already made quite a sight under the solemn oaks in Mister Pink's yard.

Bertice Sims, who was the head lady directing all, had been one of Goldie's best friends. They'd sung parts together in the church choir. She had Mangle Sanders, a church deacon, and his son Cathcart to help her with the lifting of bucks, boards, and the like. Three other ladies helped her collect the food from the women who in effect were an organised committee who baked, cooked, and fried each time one of their church family died. The word went out, and the food got collected and brought to the home, to "feed the family," they said. Those working women off at jobs and thus who couldn't do the cooking in time, made donations for the purchase of paper utensils, cups, napkins, and other store-bought things.

Most of the women had a signature food, something the community had deemed with time to be her specialty. She would be known by her special food, and this she would bring. Beauty Simmons made the best coconut pie. It tasted like the finest macaroons made anywhere in the world. Ella Mae Henderson was known for her cheese pie, made in the old way with fresh eggs, hoop cheese, butter, bread crusts, saltines, and cream. Arminta Maybin could always be counted on for her cheese biscuits kept warm in her warming pan. Willene Sims, Bertice's sister, brought a big bowl of potato salad made the way the Sims women always had. She also contributed her famous sweet potato pie. Bertice herself brought a caramel cake. All the women made a mean crispy fried chicken and country cured ham.

It was passing noon when the dinner was laid. Some Southern Brueghel would have delighted in the scene if he'd been on hand to paint it, for the tables now rose like great flowers, all brightly blossoming in the old Richards garden with their own bright blossoms of tablecloths and food.

Bertice, in her dignified, responsible way, performed her duty and let Verta May know they were at table. Reverend Jones was at table's head, ready to grace the meal. He was always at any dinner that these ladies spread and was famous for the length of his prayers. Some of the less pious men of the place vowed that the length of his graces only rivaled his appetite for chicken and ham.

Once, Arminta Maybin said she thought the flies would have carried away all the vittles before he said the longed-for Amen. Bannie Gilliam had leaned over to his friend Mangle and whispered that he was beginning to wonder whether this was a prayer or a prayer meeting that he'd gotten himself into.

The family filed out as a body, dressed in their best. Verta May with Mamie Lou and little Goldie by the hand were the first in the yard, pausing to thank in soft tones the ladies for the food and all that they'd done. Rich, with his hand on Eugene's shoulder, Vermelle, drying her eyes with a sleeve, shepherded by her tallest son, Danny, came as a group with her youngest son Beebo and daughter Madge Ernestine.

Berry and his two gangly teenage sons followed them from the door. The boys looked so self-conscious it was awkward to behold. They seldom were made to dress in white shirts and ties. Berry himself did not look comfortable in his black suit and tie. His coat was a bit tight for his shoulders that had grown with the physical labour of his job.

Taken altogether, Mister Pink's family was an impressive group, all dressed as they were in their formal best, polite, solemn, and dignified, and forming almost a processional to the tables in yard. They stood quietly while Reverend Jones blessed the food and those gathered there today.

Verta May had not forgotten to ask Triggerfoot to eat with them too. In his Sunday best, he quietly joined them there. He was walking up as Reverend Jones began his prayer, so stood at the edge of the gathering, his head bowed, hat in hand. After the Amen, he picked up a paper plate and dipped up a little food. When he'd finished walking down the long table line, he spoke to Vermelle, whose tears had begun to stream once again. As was her slow wont, she was last in the line.

"I'll shore miss him too. If he could see this today, he'd shore be proud," Trig said, trying to comfort as best he could. "Thank you for having me join y'all today."

He sat silent by Vermelle and her children on a plank seat. They were aware, without speaking, of each other's grief.

Ordinarily, Triggerfoot would have eaten a huge meal

with great gusto, for in truth, he was still just a growing boy. But today his big hands cupping the plate seemed to dwarf the little hillocks of food. His mind, like most of theirs there, was not on eating. For him, it was the solidarity of those there, a kind of extended family, that was the thing.

That was the *real* thing. Though the bonds had been strained almost to eradication by all those in the little place moving away, the community was still trying to go through the motions at least. Not being a part of it any-more, most of Pink's children and all the grandchildren had this sense lost on them, except in the back of the minds where they felt something lurking, something significant but unable to be expressed, in the soft liquid voices of the ladies and the motions of their kind gentle hands, some-thing of value they could not quite name. Verta May alone of the children fully credited the worth.

The church ladies, once the family was seated, were busy keeping their glasses filled with tea. They bustled about with great pitchers poured full from big clear-glass screw-lid jars. The condensation of water collected in jewel-like bubbles and ran down the jar walls, revealing through its silver, the amber liquid inside, the colour of Triggerfoot's hair, the colour of sun on Triggerfoot's new growing beard. It was a beard of no name, of Triggerfoot's make, a neat moustache blocked down square to his chin, kept short-clipped. He had on a crisp light blue cotton shirt and a pale tan polished sea-island cotton suit. The blue of his shirt reflected the clear bright blue of his eyes and made their hue more intense than the summer sky. His shirt collar was open. He wore no tie.

To the dark eyes around him, he looked a little like he'd stepped from the August sun. They didn't see Triggerfoot dressed up that way much, and he made an impression on them, for out in the world, he was considered handsome.

Mister Pink's children knew that Triggerfoot these past years in some ways was more Pink's child than they. Trig had needed a father, and Pink had needed a son, and he had been there to share with the old man day to day.

Pink's children understood that well enough, but still puzzled a bit why their pa chose him to say the only words at the grave, with no word from the Reverend there.

But Triggerfoot understood his friend's mind. Mister Pink trusted his friend. It was Triggerfoot whom he had taken down to the plot where he was to be buried, showing him precisely where he wanted to be put, drawing the outline with his cane. "This is where I wants to be planted," he said. "And plant me east, like all the rest of my kin, so when I sprouts, I finds the rising sun." Yes, he was to face eastward in his long sleep, like all his people gone before. Mister Pink was right to trust his friend. Triggerfoot had seen to this detail by himself helping dig the grave. And today, he'd do his best not to let his friend down.

XI

Clearing Away

~⌇∞⌇~

The dinner over and the sun now full hot to the skin, the family moved inside. The old house sat under sheltering trees. Its rooms, with their high ceilings, were surprisingly cool. A breeze blew down the hall and set the dimity curtains in motion. A few acorns left over from last year pattered on the porch's tin. It caused the Detroit lads to look up startled and think maybe someone was there.

Bertice and her friends Ascineth, Hoyalene, Della, and Arminta marshalled their efficient small army of women, who cleared the tables, cleaned and sealed things in plastic, wrapped in cloths, and covered with foil. These they brought inside to the kitchen cabinets and table for the family to have for supper when their long day was through.

Mangle Sanders supervised the breaking down and removal of the tables. These went into the back of "Old Blue," his father's 1927 Ford pickup that had now grown like a member of the family to him.

Triggerfoot apologised for not helping him, figuring

he'd as usual smudge up his clothes, and in honour of Mister Pink and knowing his part to come, wanted to keep dry and clean. He fumbled a bit nervously at a rumpled scrap of paper he'd put inside his coat pocket. Every now and then, he'd touch it to make sure it was still there.

When Verta May looked from the house door and saw Triggerfoot standing in the garden yard alone, she walked down to him, and Triggerfoot, seeing her approach, took off his hat. She invited him in. He followed her, hat in hand. These faraway children were not his neighbours, but he found sufficient bonds in a common grief.

Triggerfoot sat silent in the cool shadow of the wide hall, where the breeze cooled the sweat of his shirt. With his elbows pointed out, his back bowed, and his hands on his knees, he made his shirt like a sail. The air would soon dry him complete.

He rested in Mister Pink's favourite chair and looked at the polished coffin sitting on the little low cooling board that the Richards family, and now the Subers, always used.

It had supported the remains of Old Master and Missus before, of Berry Richards home at last in his box from the war. It had felt the weight of Suber when his own time came, of Suber's wife and grieving sister Chellie too. It had held up Goldie, and now it was shouldering Pink. Its thirsty wood had soaked up the tears of well over a century now, and these past days still soaked up more. Vermelle's were the latest. Triggerfoot wondered if hers would be the last, if the cooling board would ever hold coffin again in this hall.

The thought fell heavily upon him like a pall. It was of that, that he and Mister Pink had spoken several times on some of those late moon-drenched evenings as they rocked on the porch. Now Triggerfoot was once again alone with Mister Pink. He gazed at the polished walnut in silence, letting his thoughts drift.

His mind numbed itself in memory and remembrance, as the sounds from the various grandchildren in their rooms about the house came to him vaguely as if they'd been miles away.

Farming had taught him patience—that unwritten, silent contract for labour that circles and never ends, the same harvest, the same pulling fodder, the same seeding of the same rows, constantly attending to the same tasks that repeated and never had end.

He didn't war with time. Already, even as young as he was, he knew better than that, and instead had made peace with it. At least he didn't always think he was eternally lagging, getting behind, like some of those fashionable folks in town, who had to keep up with the day and its latest fad, fighting as they did to keep up with the progress of things. Time didn't outsmart him because he'd agreed to its slowness, its dullness and repetitions. In his country way, he'd surrendered his will to a larger design. There's no way to rush spring, or a rain, or to bring on the frost, Trig had learned from the wise. He recalled his pa's old saying, repeated often when Trig got impatient or was rushing about, "Son, slow down. World wasn't made in a day. Took six, I believe!"

So Trig sat there in Mister Pink's handmade chair, patiently waiting in silence, insulated from the shocks of the day by memory and his agreement with time.

XII

Ritual

~⟋⟍~

Then it was time, and he was back in it. Reverend Jones and eight of the choir who'd been closest to Goldie assembled on the porch and went inside. They gathered in the hall in front of the box on its board, and the women started in on a gathering hymn that had come out of their own Carolina hills: *Oh sisters, let's go down, down to the river to pray.*

The beautiful sound of the women's voices, which were always gentle and mellow, even when they raised them in anger or command, tightened the house like the goatskin of an ancient bodhran drum. The house became like an instrument itself, whose music now reverberated and serenaded fields and woods around, flowing down the valley itself to reach the bottomlands of Mister Pink's tall ripened corn, and then charming the very ripples and waves of the great grey catfish-rich river below.

As they had with Vermelle's wail of grief, the creatures of the forest stood still at this new sound, as old as the hills themselves, listening to the melody, as the men assembled now added their part: *Oh brothers, let's go down, down to the river to pray.*

The choir began swaying as it repeated its gathering chorus, keeping time to the stress of the beat, and Verta May picked up the tune. Vermelle followed in her liquid contralto. Mamie Lou's fine and clear bird-like soprano added its complement then, as the entire group there assembled, swelled the air with song: *Down. Down. Down to the river to pray.*

At the fourth repetition, Berry and Richards joined with their tenor and deep-chested base. In the fifth repetition, the words had become hypnotic; and in surprise to all, Eugene, with his own child's voice, joined in. His voice had not changed, so was the music of the clean and pure, the music of the seraphim in the voice of men.

On the sixth repetition, a few more of the grandchildren joined in, as did Triggerfoot himself, in his rich lonesome tenor, like sunlight made into sound.

Now on the seventh round, they all sang in unison, in a way to make the very house tremble as if it were one gigantic sounding board, their voices banded into one hypnotic voice, in a way to transport them from the world of sweat and care.

All felt the moment. Each had a touch, a taste of heaven's own sweetness and a glimpse of its radiant light. Here the tired would find rest, the blind see, the hurting find surcease of pain. There would be no more death on this shore. They had this promise made in the deeps of time: *Down. Down. Down to the river to pray . . .*

Mister Pink had always said that the music his people could make was surely that of the very angels of God, and all who could have heard them today would have reckoned he was right. Mister Pink wasn't much on sermons, but the proper music always could shake him, lift him, move him to tears. Triggerfoot knew that this would have pleased him, and if it already hadn't been, would have freed his soul on its way.

When Mister Pink went to the little wooden A.M.E. chapel with Goldie and the younguns, he'd sit at the open church window and look out at the fields, that is, before they put in the coloured-glass diamonds in the panes and air-conditioned the hall.

Preachers came and went. Some he liked; some he did not. They passed, but Scripture did not. Like music, Scripture moved him too. Just the reading of it could bring him around, untie the hard knot of ill-feeling to any man, and the tears of contrition would flow; but the fields that lay beyond the church's windows and doors, it was with them that he had his real understanding, and it was this that, in their frankest and tenderest moments, he had shared with young Triggerfoot. All manner of covenants, so that Trig's very head would swim. It was this that Mister Pink could not share with his own daughters and sons, not even Verta May or Mamie Lou.

So the echoes of the last repetition followed, leaving its hypnotic sway, and the house made its own instrument to serenade Mister Pink's fields.

The purple eyes of the flowers of the old man's crop of okra seemed to look wanly at the scene. Their stark and bare stalks were like the skeletons of men. This was his last crop to grow.

These straight-ploughed rows were indeed his last, and they soaked up the music's sound. They would have to store them against a long season of silence that would now be likely to fall, its shadow darkening life there on the fertile plateau.

Just at this moment, Trig remembered the offhand comment of his friend. "You know," Mister Pink had said, "you can just tell a man by the arrow-straightness of his rows." And Trig could see now, how straight indeed his friend's had been.

The cry of a far distant hawk sounded just over the hill. One who tilled and farmed the land had passed. The soil soaked up this high requiem of man and bird and would store it for yet other days, perhaps for luckier times to come.

Fallowing was part of the process, as all good farmers knew. This land might have to lie unused many seasons before it would once again yield proper fruit, and feed the bodies and spirits of men.

A redbird flew from the fig tree at the house corner. Triggerfoot watched it from the hall's open front door. The bird, feasting on the fruit there, had left tatters and shreds from which clear silver drops of sugar now oozed. A wren startled by the crowd, flew into the hall, batted lightly against a window pane then flew back out of the room, from bright into dark confusion, then back out into the sun. Trig's eye followed the wren.

Then the cousins lifted Mister Pink's box, which was easy enough, for the old man had himself become as light as a bird. As the choir sang Pink's favourite "There Is a Balm in Gilead," they shouldered him and walked solemnly down the great hall and out through the open double doors. They made their way carefully across the old porch, down steps and toward the graveyard just in sight beyond. Their exit startled another redbird, which cocked a black eye at the scene, then went back to its feast among the sheltering leaves.

The family and Triggerfoot, led by the choir and the preacher, followed behind the boys. They sang solemnly and with great feeling:

> *Sometimes I feel discouraged,*
> *And think my life's in vain.*
> *But then the Holy Spirit*
> *Revives my soul again.*
> *There is a balm in Gilead, Gilead,*
> *to make the wounded whole;*
> *There is a balm in Gilead, Gilead,*
> *to heal the sin-sick soul.*

Music like this, grown from the place, was always a part of the land. It sprang from its soil, and the soil seemed thirstily to soak up its every sound.

As the processional ended, the boys placed Mister Pink's body on the ground by the neat square of the open red grave.

All, led by the choir, sang a final song:

> *Shall we gather at the river,*
> *Where bright angel feet have trod;*
> *With its crystal tide forever,*
> *Flowing by the throne of God?*
> *Yes, we'll gather at the river,*
> *That flows by the throne of God.*

As they began their last verse, Triggerfoot stepped forward, Sunday hat still in hand, now wet where his sweating fingers had gripped.

As the last line ended, he took out his paper from the breast pocket of his coat and nervously fingered it. The paper was moist with his sweat and its ink a little blurred. There were many overscorings and interlinings. Triggerfoot had taken some time with this and had half-memorised its words. He began:

"The soil that bore Mister Pink takes him back. He comes back as a friend and is a part of it now, one and complete, and resting in peace where he never made war. He had his faults, but selfishness warn't one. His merits were many. He never deserted his own and remembered his blood, and his friends, and where he come from. He was honest and faithful, simple and pure. As his body has brought us together, may his blood remember who they are. That was to me his last words he wanted spoke at his box. Now the earth that fed him eats him in turn. And Mister Pink always knew that this is the way it should be. He told me he never regretted staying where he was born and tilling the soil. The world he saw was just a few dozen miles; but his heart didn't know no bounds, and he ranged wide in time. He didn't forget. We won't forget him. He rests among them he loved and who always loved him. And that's a fitting end for his mortal part."

Then looking up from his paper and with new words made there on the spot, Trig brought his words to an end:

"We done all we could to put him at rest the way he wanted to be. I won't say goodbye because he'll always be here. What was really Mister Pink will stay on in us who knew him and his ways."

Triggerfoot's words were slow, cleanly articulated, and dignified. They were said with the music of the place on his tongue.

Then it was Triggerfoot and Sanders who lowered the wooden box in the grave. It was Triggerfoot who threw the first shovelful of soil.

The sound of the clay striking the box echoed its base deep in the ground. Like the wooden instrument of the house echoing the singing of family and choir to serenade the fields, the box now echoed, returned back, its own deep music through the soil. The frail flesh of his sons and daughters must make of it now what they would.

XIII

Wrung Dry

~·◌·~

Then it was over. As Mister Pink had willed it, so it was done. No more words were said. As some of the family embraced and the children walked back toward the empty house, Triggerfoot noticed the simple grey gravestone of Mister Pink's father and the bright marble rose of Berry Richards, his bonded friend, parallel now in rhythm with Mister Pink's, like some continuation in time, the markers a processional ritual march of their own, the only progress that mattered here.

The sun through the cedar boughs dappled the stones with light. The summer breeze set the bright patches in motion as they played across the carved letters. Trig noticed the fall of last year's brown needles. They'd made a thin dun carpet in places on the ground.

Trig and Mangle stayed behind and covered the coffin in silence. They wanted to see that Mister Pink was properly "planted." Unlike Pink's children, Trig understood that rituals aren't much good unless you are a part of them from beginning to end. Breaking off left you unsatisfied. There was a symmetry to these things that you felt, though the mind might be unaware. The wisdom of centuries that had planned them had not planned for nought.

"What can be raised up outen this torn earth?" Triggerfoot remembered Mister Pink asking in one of his increasingly serious moods a few weeks before he died, the very same day, in fact, when he took Triggerfoot to the burial ground and pointed out where and how he wanted to be buried there.

Pink had said he'd given up on hoping for simple answers and had settled for hints and glimmerings, vague approximations, emerging out of a weave of old stories in which the tellers try to make sense of things, framing known particularities and realities, and vaulting beyond them to the realms from whence these particularities and realities all spring.

It was special how Triggerfoot closely shared both Mister Pink's seasoned wonderment and his abiding humility. He knew that the earth which Mister Pink worked all his life would now rest him, would now cradle him, and give him peace, and somehow surely would find him breath.

A lance of sunlight touched the rose on the Richards marble just the split-second Triggerfoot was about to turn his gaze toward home. The ray seemed to illumine the stone from within. Trig stopped then and stayed a moment, standing in silence, surrounded by Pink's slow, wordless fields. He hoped he'd done what Mister Pink had desired and the way he'd wanted it done. He thought he had. So did Verta May. She had said that quietly to him as she passed him after all this was done. He wished he had had more eloquence in the words he'd said over his friend, but in this he'd never been blessed, or so he felt.

Triggerfoot understood that Mister Pink knew that his dead shell of a body was all that he had to give his children at the last, and the father hoped that this would gather the children together, as many as could come, to make up the semblance of a family again, at least till they'd put him away.

The world had got splintered, fractured up, is all Pink knew. He wished it could be another way, but was helpless in that. Triggerfoot felt the great pain in his friend.

"It's a movin' age," Mister Pink had said one moonlit evening on his front porch, not too many months ago. "Even men have been on the moon and are now going to go up there to Mars."

Triggerfoot, after the usual long pause, had answered in sympathy with his friend: "Seems like everbody's movin' but nobody's really goin' anywhere. They's just chasin' their tails, like Towse did when she was a pup. But when she grew up, she quit."

Trig remembered that they laughed at this, because they both agreed that despite the incongruity of the comparison, in some ways a grownup Towse and a wise old Bleat were a heap smarter than some people they knew. The dogs at least didn't worry themselves silly in a rat race for things.

Mister Pink had recalled that his pa had told him when he got back home after the war, though he needed them badly enough, he burned his boots "'cause they'd tetched Yankee soil." After he could, he stayed on the farm and never left the county till he died. And Mister Pink said he'd done the same.

"My mamma and daddy wouldn't travel neither," Trig had replied. "And I'd just as soon stay home as not. But not so with the world around."

"Today," Trig had continued, "down here on planet earth, folks are now carrying their houses around with them in these things called motor homes."

Mister Pink added: "I wouldn't want to sleep nowhere that might be carried away in the night—go to sleep in one state and wake up in another. That wouldn't suit me none. Downright discombobulating, ding me to dignition, if it wouldn't be."

Triggerfoot had smiled his agreement. "Ding me to dignition, indeed!" The memory of that evening on the porch was as clear as if it had happened yesterday.

He now wondered how Mister Pink's children would take on his last wishes to be a family again. Indeed, how could they? That was the big question Triggerfoot had as he turned his back to the fresh mound of red soil.

He and Mangle had done a good job with the grave, and now Mister Pink was laid to rest, precisely as he'd wanted it, facing east. In this climate of quick growth, the sod would soon heal. The ferns and mosses would quickly spread.

The sun was still hot on Triggerfoot's skin as he turned heel to go. He put on his hat, slanted it that handsome way he had, then took the old worn path home.

As he did so, Trig had a vision of Mister Pink's body, animate again, slipping, dissolving into the trees where soon their green outlines too would fade with the evening mists, the fading trees by the dark river, the shade of Mister Pink standing there listening to the desperate lowing of strayed animals, needing to find their way to stables and stalls, his time-bent body propped to one side on the thinly worn hoe.

Somewhere, far away, Triggerfoot could hear the barking of beagles and the baying of hounds on a hunt, hound voices mellow and urgent, acute, the dogs probably chasing a deer disturbed out of its lair this summer afternoon. It was the sound Mister Pink had loved best of all sounds.

Then Triggerfoot thought to himself: *Soon I will wake from this dream and plough back and forth, returning and venturing out, over the cool damp autumn stubble fields of home. I will be ploughing in my rows, and Mister Pink will be ploughing in his. We will run parallel. The rows will be straight as arrows. Though we won't see each other, we'll know we're there, and both of us will be making a magic rhyme, a chant, in rhythm with our boot soles.*

With these thoughts, Triggerfoot began to sing a silent inside song that was in tune with the tread of his feet. He thought, once, then again, and yet then again, how it is a holy mystery, this feeding a man's body from the elements of soil, the very soil which had now received his friend.

It was then on his solitary walk home that the sinking feeling hit him, and how wrung dry he'd become.

His main thought was that he wanted to be alone. Vermelle's invitation to come back to Pink's with them for supper didn't appeal. He was physically tired and emotionally drained, and suddenly he had a distinct dislike for Mister Pink's children, all of them as a whole, though he didn't feel that way about any particular one.

In the aggregate, he disliked them for the pain they'd caused the old man, the pain of their leaving one by one, and not a single one to stay or settle nearby. He disliked their selfish disregard, so unlike Pink's own way.

If theirs was just the new way, as people often said, then damn the new way. If you had to travel to where the job would lead, the only way of moving up and advancing careers, he wanted no part of the game, or of this new time. It brought things, costly and perhaps even rare, but costly indeed, he felt, if bought at this price—and he didn't mean costly in dollars and cents.

These dollar and cents things were bought at too dear a cost, Triggerfoot concluded, and didn't give much happiness between. It looked to him that Mister Pink's own children were good examples of that, and a good warning to himself personally besides.

"More is what we already have," Triggerfoot declared out loud to the empty lane. "Less is what we need."

He'd continue to plough his mule. He had a new one named "Flag," and he'd not get a John Deere, certainly not mortgage his land for the sake of purchasing an expensive machine. The shiny new paint was no attraction for him, as it was for some that he knew. He didn't need an air-conditioned cab with radio music inside.

For these new windshield farmers, as Mister Pink and he called them, they had no love. The two would only shake their heads at the agri-business, agri-industry kind. They never cared for industrial farmers or factory farms. "Might as well be up there in Detroit with Berry on the assembly line," Mister Pink had said.

No, Trig would grow his corn and okra and pindars, plant his field peas, sorghum cane, and sweet tater hills just the same. Next year, he was even thinking of putting in some wheat. His watermelon patch would do glory to Mister Pink, and Mister Pink would bless his rows of tomatoes and butterbeans. His happy cows would give thick cream that Mister Pink would approve, all without the steroids that made them lactate more than nature would intend, or the resulting antibiotics to cure the infections that this would always inevitably entail. Trig knew that when you bought milk in the store in those plastic jugs, looking so neat and clean, the milk inside contained both the infection and the medicine cure for it too. He wanted no part of that scene.

Mister Pink's hand would merge with his on the hoe. The hand at the plough would be both his and the old man's. When he raised it to aim Swinge-cat to bring home the game, Mister Pink's would shadow his hand, and cock and pull trigger with him. He'd remember old Pink with each rabbit he'd skin, and often with the taste of his food.

Yes, as Mister Pink had declared in a roundabout way just a week before he died, Triggerfoot had become Pink's only son. *Needn't tell Rich and Berry 'bout that,* Triggerfoot thought, for he reckoned they already knew. That is, they ought to know, if they'd stopped and thought long enough to care.

Old Bleat was with Triggerfoot now. The last thing he'd done before he left the Richards lands was to take the long way 'round to Mister Pink's ramshackle, because seldom-used, dog pen down in the hollow out of sight of the house, and rescue the dog, where one of Mister Pink's children had sentenced him to be out of the way. There Bleat was forsaken and forlorn, sitting on his haunches, panting in the sun, waiting for what, only his dog mind could say. Maybe nothing, now that his master was dead.

When he saw Triggerfoot, he got up and looked and barely wagged his tail, not his usual vigorous wont.

"Bad business," Triggerfoot said out loud. He would have handled things a different way. So would Mister Pink.

He knew Bleat, and what a friend and companion the animal had been to the old man, especially after Goldie died. Once during the funeral, down at the grave, Triggerfoot thought he'd heard his mournful faraway howl. Or maybe that was just in his mind.

So now he got the dog out of bondage in the pen, walked him back to the fresh new mound, where both of them paused. Bleat sat on his haunches for a moment, then lay down his head on his paws, outstretched just as he'd been at Mister Pink's bed in his death watch with Triggerfoot two nights earlier, before Verta May came.

He and Bleat had Mister Pink to themselves during those

dark hours, and Triggerfoot knew certain that Bleat was aware where his master now lay beneath the sod of their home. He reckoned the scent of the old man's body, because it wasn't embalmed, was still the same, and Bleat was noted for his keenness on a deer trail. No hound in these parts could touch him. Towse for rabbit. Bleat for deer.

Triggerfoot stood there some ten minutes or so. Bleat probably would have remained lying there all night alone, but Triggerfoot called him, stroked down his head, and said to come.

Ever onward now Bleat would live out his last days at Triggerfoot's farm, and keep the company of Towse.

As the road bent to take Triggerfoot and Bleat out of sight of the old Richards place, both turned head together as if they'd planned it on cue, and took one last parting gaze.

Triggerfoot could see Preacher Jones' Cadillac leave its trail of red dirt, making a noise on the soil, and closely followed by Rich's rental car. Supper was over, and Reverend Jones was on his way home. Rich was needed back on the job in Oregon, and he'd really been gone too long as it was. He had a score of clients whose portfolios depended on him. He could, however, if he worked it right and had no airport delays, be at his desk, telephone, fax machine before noon the next day.

Berry was walking down the old steps to their car with suitcases in hand. He had to meet with lawyers about the divorce squabble, and his mind was already there. His two sons were jostling each other and trying to trip each other up in the yard. One fell into the gardenia bush, shattering blossoms and breaking a big limb. It hung there forlorn.

Verta May, Vermelle, and Mamie Lou were left to tidy up the place. They'd stay one extra day and would themselves, no doubt, in less than thirty-six hours, be gone.

Triggerfoot felt that, in all likelihood, he would never return to Mister Pink's house. He had enough of the scene. All that would have attracted him there had been laid in the clay before it had faded into the deep woods to the distant baying of beagles and hounds.

Yes, he'd have a hard time looking at the empty house. The dark window spaces of a winter evening, unlit by Mister Pink's lamp, would hurt him in some deep place within. He knew that it would and tried to put that out of his mind.

But he would now have the memory of his old friend inviolate, like the keep of a strong castle, the last place to be assailed, the place to be most fiercely defended against all.

Without someone's blessing, it didn't take much imagination to see the future at Mister Pink's. The yard would grow up in the grasses Pink had kept scrupulously cleared out. His fields would soon be overgrown. No plough would cut the soil next spring. Eventually, the pines and honeysuckle would overtake all. Triggerfoot figured the absentee owners would find no more tenants for the decaying house and run-down place. By modern standards, the old house was uninhabitable. It was drafty in winter and had only the most primitive of plumbing, no way of heating except by fireplace, and certainly no air. No one was like to give it even a second look.

As he and Bleat turned the final bend that took the house from view, Triggerfoot resolved that, yes, it would be a very long time before he'd be able to return there, if ever he could.

Trig was burned out, wrung dry. Of his own funeral, he spoke to Bleat, who turned an attentive head. "You know, Bleat," Trig said, "the more I'm around some people, the better I like dogs. I've come to a conclusion about the way I want to die and be buried out here. I want to go like Pink, suddenly, maybe sitting in the October sun, sitting on a bench with the evening sun in my face. A sharp pang, a crumpling on the ground, then my big hound to scratch out a deep hole and pull me in, cover me up, so nobody's to know, before, during, or after, and then me to heal into the soil—whole and at one. Nothing over me to show the way I went."

As if he understood, Bleat gave his companion a long wet-eyed beagle hound's look as they made their way across the hill toward home.

XIV

Home

~～☙～～

Towse met them at the crest of the hill with her usual happy yelp.yelp.yelp. Trig had told her to stay and not follow him that day, and the dog had obeyed. Now after only a five-minute walk, the two dogs already trotted along as a pair. The three entered the yard as one.

As for Triggerfoot, he had to catch up with chores he'd neglected, before night set in. He had to hunt up the eggs. His way was not the batteries of white leghorns dropping their produce into slots like squatting robots, or of cows milked by hoses and metal tubes.

The cow had wandered out of the pasture fencing and had to be brought in and milked. It was no milking at the proper time that had set her wandering outside, probably looking for Trig, if cow truth be told. She operated like clockwork, and he could tell time of the day by her wants. Usually, there was very little here to disturb the routine. It had been that way with Triggerfoot's pa and ma, and so it was with him.

He picked up his bucket and went on his way to the

barn. As the milk foamed in the shiny pail, making its splish-splash music in time, Triggerfoot, his head to old Bossy's grumbling side, thought of Mister Pink's children and how travelling about did no one good. He could smell the fresh green grass on the cow's breath.

Trig didn't know St. Thomas à Kempis' take on the matter of travel. But had he heard it, he'd have agreed. "Those who travel, seldom come home holy," Kempis had written many years ago. Or better yet, Trig may have liked the poet's declaration, *"Amer savoir, celui qu'on tire du voyage,"*— "it is only bitter knowledge that travel brings." Just then, too, he'd have understood clearly those next lines beginning, *Nous nous embaquerons sur la mer des Tenebris.*

Trig's view of travel would have harked directly back to the French root meaning of the word *travail.*

Triggerfoot gave himself up to his own simple kind of serious pondering as the milk fizzed into the filling pail.

"Them children is scattered over the whole blooming continent, from ocean to ocean, and they can get in a plane and cover it in less than a day. They think old Mister Pink was backward, hadn't seen nothing of the world. Last Christmas, *provincial* was what Mamie Lou had said he was. Reckon that's the word Baltimore librarians use."

Mister Pink had told him about her calling him this. He understood the term, and so did Trig.

Now Triggerfoot had another definition of the word, leastways a new take on it, and he'd told it to his friend. Seemed to him, there were two kinds of provincial, one of geography and one of time. Both he and Mister Pink were geographically provincial, it is true—provincials of space. No questioning this. But neither was a provincial of time. Provincials of time lived each day as if there wasn't a yesterday behind, or a tomorrow ahead, frozen in the present, atrophied, ossified that way.

"Momentary men," Mister Pink said and smiled.

Trig and Pink lived a fluid life and were not locked into the passing moment, not just living for the solitary day. Instead, they were connected to the people, past and present, who put impress on their world. They remembered and paid humble tribute outside their skin.

When Mister Pink sat in his chair, he never really sat alone. He knew that his world was a rich one for all its sparseness of things. How could he be selfish, or diminished down to the now, when he was banded, bonded in time. As he knew well, his world was big, going both back and forward in time. His horizons expanded both ways. As Trig had told him, "Mister Pink, your progress don't go just one way."

Those like Rich and Berry and Mamie, and even Verta May, thought of progress as only moving forward like the shot arrow, but really all of them were mostly locked in the now, the moment, the day, and too often in the gratification thereof. The world sanctioned their way and scorned Mister Pink's and his. So the sanctioned ones became haughty and held up their knowledge of the world and their hollow broadness as the badge of progress and smug superiority.

The insufferable pride of it all, Trig thought, *and the*

shortsighted selfishness too. These real time-provincials had no duty or responsibility to anything outside their own pampered skins. As far as rich? How funny. And how little they could see and know. A diminished world. They dwelt far below the poverty line.

Or so it seemed to Trig.

He finished the milking and led Bossy to hay in the snug stall.

"Bossy, now there is one sure enough provincial of time," Trig muttered to the barn. "And the only one I can abide, for God made her that way!"

He fed Towse and Bleat some scraps and went on his familiar path to the house, shutting gates, checking water troughs. Each repeated action fell into place and had the salutary ritual effect of gentling him back to normalcy.

As he walked to the okra patch, he wondered what he'd do without Mister Pink, for he knew the wise old man had often restrained Trig's folly and gently advised him, so he'd not have to begin each day anew, without a personal or historic memory. On this, Trig thought long as he snapped the crisp green pods from their stalks. He looked at the sweaty clothes of several days ago still draped on the old stick man and felt a tear rise in his eye.

"Pink," he said out loud.

The okra picking done, he called it a day. Good timing. The sun had just set behind the hill.

Trig's tall frame had not gotten its usual exercise, but he was mind-tired, and he felt like a sit down and rest. His head seemed to swell into his ballcap like it was just too full of the day. His emotions had drained him, so he made a simple repast.

He ate yesterday's cornbread crumbled in the rich creamy fresh milk poured up from the pail.

The old tabby that arched and rubbed its back against the open kitchen door was watching the scene. Trig poured her a saucer of heavy cream. The lamp lit her to gold as she lapped delicately with her tongue.

Trig had more than enough of yesterday morning's milk left over to churn a large golden pat of butter, about which little chore he now bent his way.

The butter soon came from Trig's rhythmical motions in little yellow specs and globs. He molded them together with his square hands into one great golden mound. For all their bigness, his hands could have a gentle enough touch.

He poured up the blue buttermilk into a Mason jar and put it in the refrigerator. Some of the remainder he put in Towse's ironstone bowl. He got out a second similar one from the corner cupboard, and that would be Bleat's. He put the rest in Bleat's bowl, an equal share or a little more.

Triggerfoot returned to his thoughts of Mister Pink's sons and grandsons, again now encapsuled in their separate worlds.

He thought of Eugene, jetting his way high over a darkened continent, rivers silver like silken threads below, mountains looking like anthills. Abstraction, telescoped distances, global village mentality, it must lead to this, and the word "provincial!" flung as carelessly as a justification of pulling up ties.

Looked at from up so high with the Olympian, godlike view, how little the particulars mattered, and how superior the flyers seemed. With such a small, supine, and helpless world, man could do as he pleased. He was indeed master of all he surveyed, or so he would think.

Eugene, who had been so painfully shy, was after only a few days at Mister Pink's already coming around. His bond with Verta May was clear to be seen. He and Trig had even had a talk about rabbit hunting, and rabbit boxes. He'd held heavy old Swinge-cat, and had begun to look for Triggerfoot and to follow him about.

He'd made a friend of Vermelle's daughter Madge. They'd gotten to comparing Oregon with Texas, and what they did at school. Cousins should be close, Trig knew. That's what cousins were supposed to be. They'd even begun to call each other Cousin Madge and Cousin Eugene.

Now all of this was broken off, no doubt to be lost for good. With no Mister Pink to bring them together, there was little practical reason to jet three thousand miles.

But blood mattered. No manner of distances and cultures and customs between, the blood ties were there and could be a firm grounding, a good foundation to make the connections that led to bonds and the proper bonding for lifetime, and all that meant. Triggerfoot mulled all of this over. He could at least hope so, for Mister Pink's sake.

It was that truth that old Mister Pink had tried to tell through Trig in his last words to his daughters and sons.

For Triggerfoot, it was a given, so obvious that this new

world, made cluttered with qualifyings of everything, had
lost the proper sight of, in its false sophistication, its ava-
lanche of bits of information, fragments of knowledge and
facts, and specialised science's hair-splitting details.

There seemed to be no sane middle ground. It was the
great disjunction of abstractions so huge and compartmen-
talisation so small that led to imprisonment in cells, walled-
in places that often took on the nature of man's self-created
world that was the likeness of hell for a man like Trig.

Triggerfoot was truly tired now. It had been a long day.
He stripped down to his shorts and lay on his back on the
cool linen of his bed. The breeze from his windows blew the
curtains out and tingled in the hair on his arms and legs.

He had grown to be a handsome fellow, they said out there
in the world. This affected him little. He expected that
maybe not being deemed so may have affected him more.

As it was, he had only one special friend of the opposite
sex. That same world accounted her beautiful, and to this
he'd say, "No argument there."

Her blue eyes were as bright as his own, and the sound
of her voice cheered him with just a word, like the growing
fields in the best growing year. Triggerfoot thought in his
fancy that her full breasts would be to him like the bosom
of earth. He saw them in his mind's eye tipped with the
tight hard bud of the rose.

Trig remembered the very words he'd said to Mister Pink
back earlier this spring. "That Becky Sue Glenn!" he'd
declared. "There's no resistin' for I'm clean gone, plumb used

up." And he could truthfully admit he was still that way.

As he looked down his long body stretched out there, he wondered how she'd feel about it, stripped like this. She was so fragile, and he so clumsy and awkward, with his big fumbling hands.

What had he to offer? He'd not gone to college, not even given it a thought. He'd take no profession, have no desk, no suit and tie, no real status in the world. He'd never have the kind of power that a big bank account brings. For all that, he cared none. He carried his power in just himself, in just who he was.

He pondered over it long, as he lay there outstretched, feeling the strength of his calves, the muscular thickness of his back and torso, the hard knot of bicep, made strong from his work.

Twenty-six and unmarried. The death of his father had for a time put marriage out of his mind. Now it was back squarely, and he'd just have to see.

He rolled his frame over on its side, and feeling now somehow a prisoner locked in this big animal cage, he curled his head onto his inner bicep, and with the new pleasant feel of bristly beard to the smoothness of skin, he fell fast asleep.

The cool breeze of a summer night blew across his frame and helped to make his sleep sound. He slept the sleep of an untroubled conscience. He'd harmed no man and had nothing of which to be ashamed. In the words of the Psalmist, he lay down in peace.

XV

A New Day

~◦~

The day after Mister Pink's funeral, Trig got up as usual just as the sky began to turn grey. After he'd milked Bossy, had breakfast, and done his other chores, he borrowed his friend Chauncey's truck and went straight into town. Becky Sue worked at the post office window, and buying stamps was a reason to go by. Legit. All legit, and he was going to ask her if he could pick her up after she got off of work at four and take her home. She usually walked to her job, living only a few short blocks away.

But Becky Sue wasn't at her usual place at the window, and this interested him some. Her friend Colie, who helped her put up the mail, told Triggerfoot she'd asked off of work today.

So Triggerfoot drove over to the Glenn house and saw no cars there. All the doors and windows were closed, but with central air this didn't mean much these days.

A rolled newspaper lay in its plastic on the brick steps to the front door. That told. They'd left early this morning, or last evening perhaps.

Rebecca Sue Glenn had just turned twenty-three, and after two years of college at the local university branch in town, had gone to work at the post office.

Triggerfoot was a high school senior when she was a freshman at the consolidated school in town there. That's how they'd met, rural youths being bussed into town; and they'd kept up their friendship over the years until now they could say they had become more than just friends.

As Triggerfoot had told Mister Pink just a few days before his death, it was time for him to put up or shut up. He'd ask Becky Sue how she felt about him. He'd be honest about how he felt about her, and would tell her straight. Pink agreed that that was the best way.

The problem was whether she'd leave a comfortable town life to take on the chores of a farm. Flies and mud. Sweat and stink. He wondered how Becky Sue would fit in. She'd been more used to pavement and grocery stores. Her father had been raised on a farm, but fled as soon as he could. He didn't even like to talk about the old days, which to them, as they declared, were certainly not "good."

And of late, Becky Sue had been talking about going to a "real" university in some big town. But she wasn't sure. She seemed at loose ends sometimes, or so Trig felt. She didn't seem to be sure about anything. Trig felt this was the case with a good many of the young women he knew.

As for Triggerfoot, towns and cities were like plants dug up and put in pots. With all the pampering and fertilising, they'd bloom to dazzle the eye, but soon die. Their flourishing would be brief. This self-loving city garden of Adonis was not for him. How ironic this was, for to some, his looks would give him title to the realm. Yet Trig was too wise for that trap, a self-destroying one for sure.

At first, when he and Becky Sue were students together, her being from town hadn't really crossed his mind, but then as their seriousness grew, it was about all that gave him doubt, so much so that, you might say, the worry began to dog his mind. He reckoned it was that fear which had kept him from declaring himself more openly or of asking such questions sooner.

Yes, he half feared her answer would not encourage him to go as far as he wanted to go. Marriage was his aim, that and a farmhouse full of younguns.

He scribbled her a note:

> *Becky,*
> *just saying hello.*
> *Trig.*

and dropped it in the shiny brass letterbox at the Glenns' front door. The plated brass lid clanged heavily as it fell and echoed its finality off the brick wall of the house pressed close next door. The sound had a tinny, hollow ring.

He stopped by the hardware to make the small purchase he needed, and then was back on the road to his own door. He was home well before noon.

Towse sensed his disappointment. Trig hardly spoke to her or to Bleat.

Trig made him a simple dinner of graham crackers and milk. By one, he was baring his back to the sun, as he chopped up some stove wood.

"Now to the fields the bronze men go," the poet had written; and without too much of a stretch, Trig, by the proper artist's hands, could be translated so.

Trig liked the flexing and tensing of his muscles. It took his mind off the world. He liked to see his body at work on its job. He was conscious of the exact way he let the axe fall or put in the wedge.

Wonder where Becky was, he thought to himself. He tried to picture her in his mind and smell the fragrance she wore.

The stove wood pile grew taller by three feet at least. It was a model of precision, stacked neatly and all in a line.

Like the straightness of ploughed rows, a tidy wood stack told something about a man, or at least that's what his pa and Mister Pink had always said. He firmly believed that too. There was no reason for Trig to question their wise observations about life. He'd never found them in error.

Winter would be coming sooner than he thought. The cold nights always had a way of sneaking up on a man, and of winter hanging on long, so it was best to start a wood pile early and labour consistently and well.

"Keep up with your work, and if possible, get a little ahead"—that was Trig's motto for the day. At other times, it was merely "Get caught up. Work hard."

He didn't mind the struggle of keeping on. It was honourable so to do, this tending God's earth and feeding God's children thereby, and it was all that he knew. Other ways might be fine for others, but this was his and his family's own. He'd always been proud to be his father's son. Their line went back over two centuries on this same land.

The soil had caused them to sweat. Its favours never came cheap, but it had never betrayed them either. His father always said that the contract went both ways.

Trig was just now beginning to learn what his pa had meant. On his own now, with no one to say him nay, and more temptations besides, it would be his time to decide whether or not to make his own pledge. It wouldn't be a light choice, and he knew that whatever it was, it would be for keeps.

XVI

Life Goes On

~ ∾ ~

Mister Pink's three daughters were now alone in the old house. Verta May had good help in sorting through Pink's few pitiful things. A lot of the threadbare clothes they mounded out back and burned. The useable garments they sorted and offered to the choir ladies at church, who received them with genuine thanks. They'd be put to good use among some of those in the community who needed them.

The girls also gave the ladies Pink's battered pots and pans. They reserved the old ironstone and Richards family things. "Antiques and folk art," said Mamie Lou cheerily. The daughters would divide these and take them home.

Most of the farm implements and tools stayed with the place, but the few things that were Mister Pink's own they put aside for Triggerfoot. He'd actually use them and appreciate them the most.

The property owner, whose name was Cromwell Frankie Potaki, made his visit to see to business in the early afternoon. He told Verta May what farm tools belonged on the place, and what did not.

Potaki had thought out loud to Verta May how hard it was going to be for him to rent out this old run-down place. He would have agreed with Berry's teenage son that it looked like a hillbilly dumping ground. He said he and his wife were rethinking their investment and would really rather sell. It might make a pine tree "plantation" for someone, and they had too much going on in town to do it themselves. He wanted fewer worries so he could concentrate on golf, and she had her bridge and canasta circles and Junior League. Truth to tell, he had been missing New York, from which he had come; and was spending more and more time going on visits back up there. A few of his closest male friends at the club suspected he might have him a young doe.

At first, their conversation made no real impression on Verta May; but Vermelle had heard it too, and said after Potaki left, "Wouldn't it be something if us children bought up this place? Potaki don't care anything for it. That's for sure. He's still a city man through and through."

Mamie Lou thought awhile. There was silence as each of the sisters pondered the thought.

Mamie Lou broke silence. "Well, it would be a place to come home to. Baltimore doesn't seem much of a home. I like my job at the library, and we enjoy the city right well, but still . . ." The pause was pregnant with a meaning all three understood.

Vermelle agreed about Houston. Verta May dittoed D.C.

"I somehow get the feeling of being cooped up in town, like Mamma's banty chickens when they were young and before she'd let them out to roam, and I can't get over it," Vermelle declared.

"Remember old Punkin, that little pony we use to ride?" Mamie Lou asked. "Remember how he'd signify on fine mornings what he felt about life. *Eeeee* he'd say, and kick out his heels behind. That's the way sometimes I used to feel. I never any more."

"Yes," Vermelle agreed, "in Houston, I don't feel that way either. Maybe we's just getting old."

"No," Verta May said seriously, shaking her head, "I think it's more."

"Trouble with lots of the city folks I'm around at the library," Mamie Lou continued, "is that for all their store-bought pleasure, they miss a whole lot of fun."

Fact is, in D.C., Verta May had come to feel the same, and from the start had always missed the pervasive little things at home, like, for example, the quiet, or the way the air smelled. It was fresh with the musky odour of the woods, of rich fern banks on creeks, the overflowed flood plain, and mossy rotting logs under moist leaf falls. She had gotten where, crossing the busy lanes of D.C. traffic on foot in front of her office building, she'd try in vain to summon up the memory of the fragrance of new-ploughed fields in spring.

It was the old tug of home. It had always been there with her, but of late, she caught herself feeling it more often, so that the thought of home was becoming her constant companion. Sometimes she had gotten to thinking that it was her only real friend in D.C. Now when threatened with the loss of that last tie owing to her father's death, she was given serious pause.

When she'd started out in her career, Verta May had visions of doing great good. Now after several decades, she'd settle for having done no great harm.

At supper that night, over casseroles, ham biscuits, rice and cream gravy, and such as was left by the church ladies from the family's funeral dinner yesterday, the three talked frank talk, while the cousins, now grown to be friends, played. One had brought a board game, and Goldie a book, which she shared by reading aloud. With her love of the printed page, she was taking after Mamie Lou.

The mothers liked what they saw. And the feel of the old house of their childhood held magic sway.

"We could own it together," said Vermelle. "Rich could buy it by himself in the blink of an eye. If the boys don't want in, maybe us girls could do."

Verta May liked the idea a lot. She could see how these three women's touch could make this a liveable, comfortable second country home. They could gather at Christmas and special times just as before. It could be boarded up the rest of the time.

"Let's ask Mr. Cromwell Frankie Potaki how much he would need," Vermelle volunteered as they and the drowsy children parted for bed. "Our family don't have much spare cash, but the boys would love fishing the river and learning how to hunt as Pappa had done."

The sisters had much to think on as they drifted to sleep. Late as it was, this was one way they could honour their pa and keep some tie to home. Without it there'd be none, and with the sisters, that was more than a sad thought of regret.

Trig's words at Mister Pink's grave followed them too. *Be true to your blood and remember who you are.*

In the middle of the night, Verta May sat bolt upright in bed. "It's the only way to keep the family together," she declared out loud.

Next morning at breakfast, the three sisters shared the thoughts they'd had through the night. It seems each of the trio had drawn similar conclusions, a fact that impressed Mamie Lou enough to say, "Seems like we better do this thing. All the signposts are pointing that way. I don't argue with dreams." At first, she had been the least enthusiastic of the three, but now she said with a smile, "Count me in!"

The breakfast was the best one they'd had yet, and after another good sleep in the quiet country dark, they now all felt a little of Punkin's *Eeeee.* Eating the same old familiar foods had had its salutary effects. As Verta May put it in her journalist's way, "The stomach sends its umbilical to its native soil." Like the house itself, the food of their youth had certainly now also exercised its own magic pull.

"What a lot of joy people miss who've never slept in the country, then eaten a good breakfast," Vermelle volunteered. "And at all seasons of the year, it's different in each. I swear, folks in the city seem to hate everything but the sun. Can't stand cloudy weather, can't stand rain, can't stand snow. Reckon they have to have it always sunny to warm up the rusty cold pistons of their hearts."

Mamie Lou said, "To hear the weatherman complain about weather for the commute, you'd think he never felt like it would have to rain. Wonder if he knows the food he eats has to have rain."

Vermelle continued, "Pa always said he liked all of nature—ice, snow, rain, a rough cold wind."

"He liked working in the summer rain, like Mr. Triggerfoot does," Mamie Lou added.

"And Pa used to remark on the heat or cold, rain or no, each and every day the Lord did send," remembered Verta May. "All seasons were beautiful and useful, he used to say. He was interested in them all. Seems to me the wickedest people in the world have to live their lives following the sun. They go to Florida or even further in winter. 'Can't stand this damn cold and snow!' they exclaim. Pa and Ma, they'd never think of not staying at home, or of finding fault with and cussing either the cold or the sun."

"At home." The words had a joyous ring, like the ringing of a fancy rare silver bell. They'd all gotten over the pull of city life, and, if truth be said, maybe just a little sick to death, of the picturesque far away.

XVII

Plans

~◦~

Vermelle stayed at the house picking the okra. She had on her ma's garden gloves against the itch and sting of the spiny pods. As she picked, she hummed and sang a little childhood tune she'd learned at her mamma's knee:

Whatcha gonna do when the meat give out?
Stand in the cawna with your chin poked out.
Whatcha gonna do when the meat come in?
Stand in the cawna with a greezy chin.

She was tending the children so Verta May and Mamie Lou could drive into town—that is, to one of its immaculately redundant subdivisions that even this small village had begun to spawn. Here at the most fashionable suburban address, the chemicals went down on the lawns every Saturday, riding mowers made noise and fumes, the sprinklers pumped full blast every summer night. Grass clippings and leaves were hermetically sealed in black plastic bags and sat neatly at the curb—like soldiers at attention in this war to make the world safe for the smug and tidy, or so it seemed. Here on these manicured lots the birds had quit coming around and the rabbits had exited, having no cover or place to nest.

Here, along these streets, there was no sign of life. The people stayed mainly inside, hurrying from air-conditioned car to air-conditioned house, and air-conditioned house to air-conditioned car to air-conditioned workplaces or malls, the shoe soles never touching soil.

It reminded Vermelle of what Triggerfoot had just said about not caring for the new factory farmers and their industrial farms. They were taking the day, but to him it was a bad sign, like the sprawl of housing developments across what once used to be farmland, orchards, and pastureland.

The sisters found Mrs. Cromwell Frankie Potaki at the address the couple currently called home: Number 33 Arcady Lane. She had just returned from taking their teenage daughter to the swimming pool. She said Frankie was out at the moment on chores on his way home from the club, but would soon be back.

Mrs. Potaki invited them in through the kitchen into the den. It was one of those cathedral ceiling great room affairs with exposed fake wood rafters in between insulating Celotex squares. From the "cathedral" peak, instead of a cross, hung a great white ceiling fan, like a giant airplane propeller, that blew down hot air on the three women there. Mrs. Potaki's neatly, elaborately coiffed hair did not stir. For all the world, it looked to

Verta May like a garden-club flower arrangement.

The Cromwell Frankie Potakis collected things. There were mini-collections everywhere: Mrs. Potaki's Doughty Bird porcelains, Frankie's antique toys, Mrs. Potaki's Hummel figurines, Frankie's Civil War swords, Mrs. Potaki's Canton Export china and Japanese screens.

Copies of *Southern Accents* and *Colonial Homes* lay scattered on polished and primitive tables of old heart pine, cherry, and walnut.

A pegged local-made pine sideboard was Mrs. Potaki's newest find. It had been painted with an indigo stain, but since this didn't satisfy her craving for wood grain, she'd had it stripped and sanded, then polyurethaned.

There it sat shining on the deep pile of shag carpet as if the toes of its tapered tall legs didn't want the meeting but had become reconciled to having to share this manufactured scene.

On the top of the sideboard were spread the invitations to a dinner party she was about to throw. Mrs. Potaki was almost through with the chore of addressing them and sending them out.

The sound of tires on the pea gravel outside announced someone in a hurry had just arrived. The car had come to a quick halt, making the gravel grate and pop in raucous complaint.

Mr. Potaki soon came in the front, letting the door slam. "Ladies," he said, as he passed briskly to the rear. He had his leather golf bag slung on his left shoulder and a six-pack of beer gripped by the plastic collar on his right hand. His face was red over his tan golf shirt that showed the bulge of belly that was becoming a paunch. He didn't come in through the triple-car garage at the back because he was going out once again. Down the hall, through the front windows, Verta May could see the shiny white Lincoln on the pea gravel arc at the front door.

To the refrigerator the beer went. That could not wait.

The distant sound of water from the half bath of their mudroom, and Frankie returned shortly, sans golf bag and beer. He was obviously pressed for time. He usually was.

"What can I do for you guys?" he asked.

"We were wondering what you'd want for Daddy's old house and the forty-eight acres of land," Verta May brought the question straight to a head. She'd learned with his sort of folks that this was usually the best way. She'd been around the block in D.C.

"Well now," he figured. "Land without grown timber that's cutable in those parts sells at about a thousand an acre, no less. Where it is, out in the middle of nowhere, I calculate the house isn't worth a thing, unless you could sell it and move it away, to restore it in town, or maybe to be dismantled for its old heart pine. Otherwise, in fact, it would cost something for a bulldozer to take it down. How about an even fifty thousand? I think that would do. How about that, sweetums?" he asked his wife.

"It's your sphere," Mrs. Potaki replied. "Fine with me. I never knew why you wanted to buy it anyway. The

Sinkewitzes were certainly glad to unload it on us. They'd gotten tired of dabbling in the picturesque, in the 'local colour,' as they said." Verta May figured Mrs. Potaki didn't even realize what she'd just said.

The Sinkewitzes were from New Haven, Connecticut, and had come South many years before the Potakis had. By "local colour," they meant anything faintly rural, and that usually meant coloured folks too.

"How about forty?" Verta May countered as she looked at Mamie Lou.

Mamie Lou added, "Mr. Potaki, we're just two women. We couldn't farm. You know women do farm work but don't ever farm." Verta May resisted the inclination to smile. Her baby sister was a subtle one.

"Well, let's halve the difference. Make it forty-five, and it's yours," he said. "We're tired of the place, seldom even go out there. Now that they'll be no more vegetables and hams for our parties, I can't even see one reason to delay. But it could be a real beauty with an outlay of about two hundred grand—that is, if it wasn't so damned far away from everything."

"The real boonies," Mrs. Potaki chimed in. She was thumbing the new issue of *Antiques Magazine* the postman had just delivered this morning.

Potaki continued. "The old house was built about 1825, they say."

"Could make *Southern Living* or *Colonial Homes* if properly restored," added Mrs. Potaki, and she glanced from her

Antiques to eye copies of these magazines lying on the pegged pine table, Georgia Piedmont, circa 1810.

"Such as it was, it was our home, where we two were born," Verta May returned.

"We're interested and will let you know," Mamie Lou said. "Thank y'all for inviting us in, and for your time. Time's money, as I guess you know."

And the two sisters went out and into their car on their way. They didn't let their excitement show.

"Are we crazy?" asked Mamie Lou.

"Probably," answered Verta May. "We need that old falling-down house like a hole in the head."

"And we can't be interested in the 'local colour,'" Mamie returned, "'Cause we're it. Maybe not quite local enough to qualify though. Wonder if we're picturesque?"

Verta May smiled. Yes, she'd always liked her sister's dry sense of humor, the thing that always set her apart, even when a child.

"Maybe we should have shown up at Mrs. Potaki's eating big slices of one of Pa's watermelons," she declared. At that, they both had a good laugh.

As the car rolled through the familiar lanes of town and then into the countryside, they both felt freed—in some strange way, released from a vague dread, some nagging chore which they could not name. But with this house, they knew they'd be taking on more new chores in addition to the vague ones that nagged. Still, this didn't seem to dampen their spirits. It served to give the incentive of adventure and challenge to the undertaking. Both thrived on challenge too. They were the daughters who were most alike that way.

Verta May, in particular, felt the old tug of home, and the life she'd led there. It involved getting up early, and physical labouring too, but what you did always mattered. You could see the results, and right away. If you didn't do such and such a thing, the food for the winter was not there. People went hungry or got fed in tune with your actions accordingly. If the cow wasn't milked, she went dry, and real hardship loomed. In this world, unlike her announcing job in D.C., talk was not the key. At this, she remembered her pa's saying that talking and doing don't lie down together much. She was beginning to understand that learning theory before practice was the bane of the modern world. One of her learned journalist Ivy League colleagues was always quoting Heraklitus that words live longer than deeds, but she knew her pa would qualify that. He would no doubt add that for the words to matter at all, they'd have to have the test of deeds behind them. That was the wisdom of a country way.

Here on the land, it was doing that prevailed. And personally, she'd about had enough of what she was beginning to consider as hot air, if not downright lies. She didn't like the way words could be twisted to lie without people getting caught. She was respected in what she did. She had liberty to voice truth as she saw it. Liberty she defined as the right to tell people what they don't want to hear. Of late, she was becoming the exception in this, not the rule. Yet, still, she had the liberty to do her work her way.

But this direct connection of cause to effect was often still missing in much that she did. It had affected the way her whole life had become. There was a disconnect she was trying to put her finger on.

All she knew clearly was that she often felt numbed and sometimes not quite alive, as if living in a yellow fog, an ether that was more than that from the pollution of cars. And she longed for honesty, an honesty beyond liberty to say. She wanted that honesty all around. She missed it horribly. She craved it more and more.

Yes, she was feeling the old tug of home and didn't want to give up that last tie. She was, in addition, even more so feeling the enjoyment of riding with her baby sister and sharing the humour they'd always enjoyed. With no husband, or prospects for one, and no children besides, she was becoming more and more conscious of being alone. And in a city, loneliness without a family could cut like a knife. She'd learned to deal with it. Now, however, she was beginning to wonder why she had. Was it worth the pain?

But a bigger question at hand now loomed: How would Vermelle take all this when they returned home?

XVIII

Agreed

They didn't have long to wait to find out, for twenty minutes brought Mamie Lou's dusty Chevy Chevelle into the clay arc and under the sheltering limbs of the old carriage drive.

Vermelle, in fact all of them, thought the price good, being used to real estate prices in Baltimore, Houston, and D.C. where forty-five thousand wouldn't buy a decent condo in a one of the three. And this house had forty-eight acres of land with it.

None of Mister Pink's family had ever owned legal title to any land before. They'd in a sense owned it, but their kind of ownership didn't record in the big leather-bound ledgers at the county courthouse. And it didn't keep them from being put out of their home at someone else's whim. Knowing that had to do something to a person. How could he feel independent then?

Now, it wasn't the idea that impressed Vermelle, but the reality of the thing.

"You know, I really enjoyed picking Pa's okra," she said. "If I'd used a long-sleeved shirt with my gloves, as Pa always taught, my arms wouldn't be itching like crazy now, and then it would have really been perfect fun."

Vermelle remembered that Mister Pink had left a few stalks in the fall, so they could run up to seed. He'd pick the big blackened pods and strip out the little black beads that were shiny as glass. It was seed that his own father and fathers before had always gathered each winter and fall.

Picking the okra brought back her girlhood. That was one of her chores from twelve years old till she left home.

Today she had one of her pa's split-oak baskets full, mounded high with the bright green pods. She'd already put a pot of it on to boil. And the rest, she'd dice up, flour, and fry.

It was a taste out of their youth all three of the women longed for. The stylish of the day would call it "comfort food." And other than a few spongy blackening pods, okra could not be had in even the exclusive specialty markets of their towns. The world had not yet come to okra, it seemed.

As a matter of fact, Vermelle had never really liked Houston or taken to city life. As she often said, she felt "cooped up" there. Houston was too flat and crowded, and was too big for her. She missed the deep shade of forests and cool winding paths green with mosses and ferns.

She liked to ramble at will, unseen, walking where her fancy led and not stopped by traffic, curbs, or property lines. Yes, she'd like a place to come to, which she could call home, and maybe return to one day for good.

"I could scrape ten thousand together, I expect, but I'd have to sell this idea to Dawk. Maybe if Rich would chip in ten thousand and you two girls, that would make most of the sale."

Her boys, overhearing, clamored for them to do it, "Right now, Mamma. Right now!" They'd like to hunt rabbits with Mister Trig straightaway, and learn how to plough. They wanted to go fishing in the Broad like Grandpa had taught them to do.

So the three women could talk only of their plan until bedtime had come. At this crucial point in time brought on by their pa's death, they'd again become one, and now had about decided to take on the scheme. Their lives had seemed to change drastically almost overnight.

Mamie Lou recalled a conversation she'd had with Triggerfoot back last year. It had made an impression on her then, and was coming in handy now. Trig had said, "You know, Miss Mamie, one reason a farm fails is that the farmer feels he's got to live up to city folks' ways and have all the conveniences they have. Farm life cain't be citified that way, and still be a farm—not to mention stay out of debt and last. That kind of a farmer has give up from the start, and he might as well pack his bags and work in a mill. Would save him and his poor family all the agony of slow wasting away."

Verta May and Vermelle listened intently and understood the message. They knew Triggerfoot spoke the truth.

They'd keep the farm rural, not make it a factory farm, not a city place. That is, if the sisters decided to go through with the plan, and it looked now like they would.

In her mind, Verta May in the car on her way back home from town had already decided that if the others backed out, she could go it alone. Single, as she was, and with a good job, and no real expenses (her health had always been good, and she never visited a doctor, not even once a year), she had put away quite a tidy sum, which she had invested soundly and well. It would not even make a major dent in her portfolio to write a check for three times the sum of the entire purchase price.

But if the sisters wanted in, she wanted them in too. It would be the icing on the cake to have them involved. Not four days ago they were in separate worlds, and now their lives once again had already converged into one.

"Y'all, let's do it," she urged.

The aura of small, local places included their timelessness, Verta May had come to conclude; but she was also coming to realise that only those who stay in these places are privileged to have that perception. For those like herself who've left and periodically pop in on brief returns, the sense of change is dramatic. They'd witness aging in the faces of those they hadn't seen in three or four years. They'd see the marks and scars of change that those who stay rooted there within time do not. Not so with them, those who lived inside time.

She'd perhaps like to be one of those who also lived

within time, in the heavy velvet folds of time's cloak, never witnessing the rawness of its shocks and ravages and losses, easing by slow stages into eternity.

What were these thoughts? She'd never had such before or in such a tone of seriousness in the pursuit of her career. This was a new thing for her, and she wondered from what source it sprang. She didn't know yet whether she liked it in herself or not. She figured it would finally have the end result of inconveniencing her safe and comfortable cocoon of a life.

She said goodnight, yawned wide behind the back of her hand, and went to her bed, putting the thoughts away. She was tired out from the labours of the day and would sleep well and long.

XIX

The Grapevine

When Triggerfoot heard that Verta May and her sisters had put down earnest money on the neighbouring farm, he had mixed feelings, but was mainly pleased. He wanted the place tilled, not left deserted to grow up in pines, and he hoped Verta May had not done this as a lark. The land was good. It had once been a fine farm, as his daddy had told him, one of the finest around, and would be again if only the right ones would take it on. He wondered if Mister Pink's daughters were the right ones. Yes, he had his doubts.

Still, he was glad that Mister Pink's blood would own title to the place, as the old man never had. He just wished the children had done this a decade ago, so Pink could have worked on his own land.

Not that he had worked any less hard on his jobs. Triggerfoot wished he had just had the satisfaction of knowing that he didn't do things on shares and that he couldn't have been made to move at any year's notice.

If that had happened, where would Mister Pink have

gone? Triggerfoot knew that at his age, it would have likely killed him to go to a home or live with one of his chaps in a big town.

But Mister Pink had never worried. He had faith; and a kind Providence, and the run-down, bedraggled nature of the old place out there forgotten by the world on its old rutted dirt road had been his protectors in this. Very few people even knew it was there. Since nobody envied it, the world had let it and Mister Pink alone. Lucky he was. Many whom Trig had known were not so lucky as he.

Still, yes, he wished the chaps had acted while Mister Pink was alive.

"What a present they could have give him one Christmastide!" Trig said out loud to his walls.

At his voice, Towse and Bleat perked up their ears, hoping he was saying "Let's go out. Let's go get rabbits or deer."

The sisters had all gone their ways now, but had left the earnest money behind. The Potakis insisted on a realtor to do all the paperwork, so the word quickly got out.

It was heard all about town, but hardly made a blip on the radar of the town scene. Yes, the old Richards place was so far out in the country that, to most, it hardly existed. Those who knew of it at all wondered in amaze why the Sinkewitzes and Potakis had ever wanted the place. As for Mister Pink, if they'd known he ever existed, they'd thought by now, he must have died.

So the grapevine brought Trig fairly accurate news.

Verta May herself had hinted as much the day she came by with a few of Mister Pink's woodworking tools to give to him "to remember him by." A nice gesture this, friendly and appreciated by Trig.

"Much obliged," he said. But forget Mister Pink? He'd not need tools to remember him by.

They were Pink's froe and drawing knife. Trig had recently set himself to making a few baskets out of split oak. Trig remembered the craft from watching Pink many a time, and crude as these first ones were, he already showed promise in the skill. Mister Pink's sharp drawing knife would help.

On the day Verta May brought him the tools, Trig departed from his usual good manners in times like this and made one request. "If y'all wouldn't mind me having Mister Pink's blue chair, I'd be much obliged," he said. The children complied, and Trig straightaway put it at his hearth right by his own.

Verta May left four days after the funeral, staying on one more day past Vermelle and two past Mamie Lou. She wanted the place to herself for a time.

Triggerfoot understood very well the desire. She, like himself, was quite happy alone, was used to it in fact, and needed to be by herself to think things through.

Like him, she too had a very rich inner world. Living solitary had required it of her. It was filled with things of her mind's making and musings that few would ever know. Rich, very rich, indeed.

In the meantime, Triggerfoot had found Becky Sue.

After a long four-day weekend at Edisto Beach with her parents at the Glenns' old screened porch beach house, she and her father, mother, and brother were back home.

She looked more beautiful than ever in her blush of tan there at the window of the P. O. The sun had tipped her light brown hair with flaxen tones. It always did that when she got out in the sun. God, she clean took his breath away.

Trig took her out. They did some pretty heavy kissing, and stopping at their favourite quiet spot on the way home, she accepted the ring he offered when he asked her to marry him.

"Oh, Trig," she said. "Of course I will." Twenty-six and unmarried. Yes, it was high time for him.

Life was again good for Trig. He was, as in the cliche of song, walking on sunshine, walking on air. Everything looked bright and richly new to him. He'd never seen things exactly this way before. He only wished he could tell the news to his father or to Pink, share his joy with them, someone besides Towse and old Bleat. Saying it to Mister Pink's grave wasn't the same.

It was then he realised a truth that he felt everyone must come to and know in the end—that grief over loss of loved ones was more for oneself and missing the grieved than for the loved ones who'd gone on before. Especially those like Pa and Mister Pink, who were gentle, fine men, and had gone to their reward.

It was hard for Trig to accept this essential selfishness of grief, but Old Stephney knew it, there in her sable robes in

Mister Pink's old locked-up, boarded-up house, where she now was the Missus and Master besides.

He imagined her sitting in one of Mister Pink's rockers just inside the hall door. One evening as he walked by the dark empty house on his way to Mister Pink's grave, he sensed her cold eyes watching him above the shrunken, toothless mouth, as an omen that his happiness would not be forever, as indeed it was never for all mortals below.

XX

Consequences
~ ∾ ~

And, true, the happiness did not last long with Becky Sue and him. She gave back his ring three weeks and five days later when it became clear to her that her fiancé would never move to town.

As for herself, she never dreamed of living "out there." She'd no idea he expected her to. She thought he'd be getting a real job, a town job, and doing something with his life.

Triggerfoot should have known. He felt like kicking himself for being so blind. What a fool! But all he could see was a shimmering bright Becky Sue. Her beauty was enough to blind to everything else.

"But I should have known," Trig kept mumbling to himself. One evening on the old porch swing at the Glenn house in town, Becky had asked him what he'd do if he had a million dollars. This was the kind of dreaming she loved to play as a game.

After a little thought on the matter, Trig had said, "A million dollars? Reckon I'd just keep on farming till all of it was gone." He smiled and squeezed her hand.

He was half in jest, half in earnest, but Becky Sue didn't smile. He aimed a kiss at her, but she turned her face so as to prevent it. Right then, he should have known. It was coming clear to him now just how far she had been from being amused. Maybe if he'd been thinking straight and not blinded, this should have told him all he needed to know.

Later, he had thought bitterly to himself that the money most folks strive for had the proper images on it.

"Every piece of it," he mumbled, "has a face to each backside and a backside to each face." He laughed out loud at that, and wished he had Mister Pink to share the jest.

No, he and Pink traded and bartered with everyone whenever they could or just gave things away. The state's currency always sat uncomfortably in pocket or hand.

He understood the wage earner's comfort in having a weekly paycheck. There was assurance in that, Becky Sue was quick to remind. "God don't pay on Fridays," he'd told her then, remembering the saying from his pa. He wondered now if she even had the slightest clue as to what he meant. It went further than farming's being a partnership with God.

But Becky liked everything set and in a pattern. She wanted everything to run smoothly and be in its place. In that way, she took more after her mother than her dad, who was more relaxed and believed it was best just to live and let live. Mrs. Glenn ran a tight ship. She was part of the society of the place. In that, she may have overdone it, over-compensating because she wasn't born to it. She was an

Austen from Greenville. Her parents had moved there from England to help set up one of the new plants that were springing up like toadstools after a rain. In liking cities and wanting to impress man's ways upon the world, Becky was clearly her mother's child.

As for Trig, just being in town so much of late with Becky Sue had made him feel that he was beginning to detect the signs in his own life of a creeping insulation, a kind of sealing-off abstracting process that blurred his image of the land and of other human beings. He felt it in the plastic facelessness of the town scene, the too much money coldly and unconcernedly passing hands there, the new interstate highway just built, the too many cars and the regimentation they required, the bulldozed earth, the big conglomerate chain stores, the fast-food restaurants, the sprawl of cookie-cutter subdivisions, the impersonality of it all, in a virtual McWorld.

Or so it seemed on the September day Becky Sue had given him his ring back.

Before she did, he should have known it was coming, because she had that serious, businesslike look she sometimes could wear. She started in on a conversation she and her mother had had the other day. Her mother had said that culture is a thing of accomplishments and the mind, and that she should go back to college. Becky was not impressed when Trig told her that her mother might be right but that he'd always thought culture was a thing of the heart.

One thing led to another, and almost in shock, he was

left standing on the porch by himself with the little ring box in his hand.

And the day had started out so promising. There was a bright clear sky as the sun climbed over the mists. The trees on his farm materialised out of the fog, roosters crowed, and dogs barked as he'd started out on his dirt driveway. He was in such high spirits as he drove onto the asphalt of town.

No, Becky had said. She'd just have to give him his ring back while she had time to think. Her mother had said that before she even thought of marriage, she ought to study for a career. She had to think about that. She made it clear, however, that she didn't say no, provided he would change his mind about getting a job in town, or in some town. In fact, a bigger one would suit her better anyway, one with a real college, not the branch university campus here.

This wrenched Triggerfoot's heart and tore at him in the way he'd felt first when his mother and father died and then recently at his old friend's passing just six weeks before. Oh, how he needed to talk to one of them now.

A firm no would probably have been better for him. As it was, Becky's blue eyes and beautiful form were like Dante's Beatrice, leading him on, but never allowing a touch, never fulfilling the cravings of a healthy young fellow's body, yearnings that were natural to him and for which he was rightly not ashamed.

"It most surely is a thing of the heart," he declared to himself some days later. He wondered why Becky couldn't see that. He'd certainly be true to her.

Now he lay on his bed and watched his bare chest rise and fall in the rhythm of breath. He considered the strong legs and arms and wondered what Becky was doing and seeing this night. He could smell in his mind the fragrance she wore. The light of a full harvest moon through the open window fell on him there. Old people said that a young couple who slept in a full moon's light would surely conceive and that it would be a man-child. A son to follow his father's plough.

He looked at his long body and wondered why he was made, what for, if not for Becky and tilling this land, a land so fertile and willing to be tilled.

Old Stephney had warned him from Mister Pink's boarded-up house. He remembered her there, and her aged and wizened hooded form now merged with the freshness of Becky Sue's in his mind. Happiness, loss and grief. Grief and loss. He knew it once more.

The chill of the air now caused him to pull up the linen sheet over his nakedness.

"Sleeping alone one year more," he said to himself, as he shut out the full moon's light by turning his face to the wall. It fell across the white hills and valleys his body made beneath the sheet.

From a distance, he could hear beagles baying on a trail. Hound voices from far off. Their mingled calls were accompanied by the fast and furious whoops and hollers of the drivers. It was the sound out of nature that he always liked best, that both his father and Mister Pink liked best too—that and a bobwhite's clear clarion call and the first whippoorwill's crystal note in the spring.

The memories of all these had a music to soothe his hurt soul. He wouldn't give up on Becky Sue, not just yet, maybe never. After all, she hadn't said no.

"God don't pay on Fridays," he said out loud to the dark. "And a man shouldn't try to be better than God. It's just when he does that he makes a ice of himself and all hell breaks loose."

Yes, he'd try Becky once again, but he'd made one final decision too. He'd be true to this place of his blood, and not move in to town—this town, or any other town—Becky Sue or no. Like Vermelle had said of Houston, he felt cooped up there. This aching big body would not make him betray.

XXI

Limbo

~ ∾ ~

When Becky Sue put him off again, it occasioned a harsh exchange or two, the harshest words Trig had ever spoken to her. They'd just been lost in a long kiss there on her porch swing. The touch of her firm breasts to his shirt made his senses swim. Both of them had been deep in the moment, so how could she put him off so? She'd brought him up so high, just to dash him down cold again.

It was like the cold shower you were supposed to take. How much more of that could he stand? Did she love him or not? He wanted her in the worst way. Did she want him?

Other than this career and city stuff, they got along so well. They truly enjoyed being with each other.

Trig was mainly just puzzled by it all. Harsh words turned to a real full-blown row, and he'd gotten red-faced and angry. His fair skin was a quick register for his feeling anyway. And in this, the red of his passion just minutes before turned to the red of anger now. When he got mad or excited his blue eyes flashed in a way that couldn't be explained. And the sight of that now actually frightened Becky Sue.

She just got up, turned her back to him, slammed the screen door, and went inside, leaving him sitting outside on her daddy's porch alone, yes, red-faced and mad, feeling like a fool.

At the door's slam, he could hear Mr. Glenn from deep in the den call out over the noise of the TV, "Beck? Everything all right out there with y'all?"

Most certainly, everything was not, at least from Trig's view.

He walked awkwardly away. He noticed that she didn't even watch through the curtains.

He choked the car cranking it up.

When Trig got home in the dark, it took him his chores and more than an hour on his own dark porch to cool down.

Even Towse and Bleat knew to leave him alone, and lay down to themselves in another room.

The next morning, Triggerfoot was early at work in the cornfield, pulling the last ears of dried corn, which he piled in the split-oak cotton basket at the end of the row. These he hoisted with one strong arm onto his shoulder and poured into the filling corncrib.

The gold of the bounty served to soothe him some, but still flits of anger came across his face. His face reddened, and the anger flared.

Early in the afternoon, Trig laid his back to the chopping of his winter wood. The pump of blood into his flexed muscles made his flannel shirt tight across his shoulders.

As the axe bit the wood, it made a solid ring, and he hummed a little song of accompaniment by a singer named Dave Coe he'd liked to hear on the radio—a tune that told of having a wood burnin' stove and no natural gas, with the chorus repeating, "and if that ain't country, I'll kiss your ice."

That about summed up his attitude today pretty well. Trig vowed that the only natural gas he'd have around the place would be natural indeed, and especially after a supper of black-eyed peas.

Exaggerating Coe's own drawl, he made his own Upcountryman's *ice* louder and more distinct in further rebellion against the droned monotone of the urbanised world's scorn of all things rural, and its precious and deadly, prissy way.

As he wedged and chopped, and hummed his song, Trig's eyes continually danced and occasionally flashed in their electric way. They hinted at a mischievous nature kept down by the serious need for Becky Sue. Eventually, under the right circumstances, that true nature of his had the potential to break free and make itself known. The future would tell.

In the midst of his work, Vermelle and Verta May drove over to tell him they'd closed on the farm. They had bought it outright, and it was now legally theirs, as the courthouse documents would show: the property of Vermelle, Verta May, Mamie Lou, and Berry. They hoped Mister Trig would be glad.

Verta May laughed to Triggerfoot: "Wasn't gonna lose the chance to have the best watermelons in the whole wide world." She remembered how Triggerfoot had laughed when she told the AMTRAK story to him and her pa years ago.

Yes, they repeated, they hoped Mister Trig would be glad they'd bought their daddy's farm. They'd try to farm it right, and be good neighbours, that is, when they were around, if in that, good neighbouring would be possible. But, in time, they felt they'd be more and more here, and less and less away.

Verta May had worked out a deal with her station manager that she could do up her Op Ed pieces and phone them in, or tape them ahead in lots. That way she'd be able to spend a good deal of time on the farm—weeks at a time, sometimes a month—and maybe could get the fields ready to farm in the coming spring. They'd just have to see.

Vermelle was sending her two stalwart young teenage lads for the three months they were out of school next summer to help Verta May out. They were raring eager for that, and Vermelle hoped Mister Trig would take them under his wing. Above all, they wanted to hunt.

"Not want them to be a big bother though," Vermelle said to Trig, "But y'all seemed to hit it off the last couple times we were here. Even in Texas, all they do is talk about you."

Trig answered "Shorely." He'd like to have them along on his hunts and maybe they could use Mister Pink's and Pink's daddy's old guns he'd given several years before he'd died. The lads could hunt old Bleat, who, despite his age, had plenty spunk left in him yet.

"That would have sure pleased Mister Pink," he told Vermelle.

At that her eyes teared. Trig sensed regret in that—of all the little things that might have been done when there was still time.

"Time . . . time," Trig mumbled to himself after she had gone. The words came in rhythm to the lift and fall of the axe. "Time . . . time."

Yes, Vermelle was okay, and her sons were tall, strong, broad-shouldered lads, like their Suber line. They could help bring the place back, if they would. If they didn't lose interest, he could see making real farmers out of them.

"But you know children nowadays," he said to himself. "They have the attention span of gnats."

Triggerfoot needed this new focus as a diversion from his disappointment and turmoil with Becky Sue. Against that, his wood chopping done for the day, he turned in the late afternoon to fodder pulling in his autumn fields—one of the least enjoyable chores of the farm cycle year. It was downright onerous labour as all who've done it know.

Given his state of mind, that's why he chose that particular job to do. Its roughness seemed to match his mood. He relished the harsh work today. "That Becky Sue!" He hoped the dry corn fodder would slice and cut.

Despite the heat of the sun this more than usually warm late autumn day, he wore the heaviest flannel shirt that he had, over an undershirt too, collar buttoned high up as possible, with a red bandana tied around his neck. He wore his thickest jeans and high-topped Red Wing boots over tall woolen socks. At least he'd sweat out some of the pain.

Even with all this armor of clothes, the dry sharp fodder blades still cut round his gloves and left marks and thin trickles of blood on his forehead and cheeks. The dust of the fodder choked him, and he had to put the bandana over his nose.

He tore into this job with a pent-up energy that took some hours of steady work to take off his edge. But the work, preceded as it was by a vigorous go at the axe, finally wore him down, and at last he regained even keel. His mind was numbed and his body on automatic.

In the process, he woke up amazed to see the plenty of stacked wood and the fodder he'd stacked into neat piles, quite enough to keep Bossy and Flag to last out the winter, and perhaps some left over besides.

The brown ricks after the full day made picturesque teepees in his fields, and the neatly stacked wood did his heart good.

Yes, his energies now spent, he could gentle down.

It was time for supper, and he had a big piece of venison left over from yesterday's roasting spit. He'd killed the buck on the edge of his woods. It had weighed near two hundred pounds.

He said a blessing his pa had taught and thought of the sleek soft-hided deer that had given his life for this meal. He pictured the heavy rack, like some strange tree in a fantasy world. The brown juices ran from the strong-tasting meat. Triggerfoot thought as he relished his food: *Yes, a cannibal world.*

Trig respected the food he ate, raised from the ground or killed in his woods. He ate for survival but ceremonially too, and at times with ritual care. He accepted the curse that all of creation—man, beast, fowl, fish, and herb—must live off other things, and that only by ceremony could he soften and make bearable such knowledge of how he must live.

He thought back to the cornrows he'd harvested this morn. As always, he'd left some corn ears and nubbins scattered in his harvest rows. The bobwhites, he knew, needed these to survive. He thought of them now, scratching and scrambling hard to find food to sustain them, like all things had to do. He reckoned himself among them. But the birds' habitat and food sources had dwindled down severely of late, and so Trig did his little bit to help them survive.

What with fire ants about to come on the scene devouring their young, and even eating into their eggs, they'd have quite a struggle, as if everything kept on conspiring against them these days.

What poverty the world would suffer, Trig thought, if these birds were to be no more.

Last spring, he'd planted a couple patches of lespedeza and some yellow partridge pea just for them. Mister Pink and he talked about that, and Mister Pink had smiled and approved. Trig's mind now focussed on next year's lespedeza plantings he'd make time to do.

Maybe Vermelle's boys would take an interest in helping him work with the bobwhites. They had shown the inclination to learn when he watched them about Pink's place on their short flying visits from Houston last couple of years.

Trig liked their big Texas hats. They asked all the right questions, and he took this as a good sign. But he knew they'd have their hands full at Pink's, especially these first few years of getting things straight.

He wished he had sons of his own.

"But back off of that thought," he said to himself. "Better back off of thinking of that right now, or I'll get mad," and a flush of red crossed his forehead and cheeks and lingered some time before it was gone.

Yes, these boys might work out. When Vermelle had driven over today, she had brought Trig a present the boys had sent. It was a broad-brimmed Texas "summer hat" like the ones that they wore and he admired. They picked up somehow that Triggerfoot had liked the way their hats shaded out the sun and cooled their heads with the white mesh. Now he had one of his own, from that far-off cowboy land he knew he'd never see.

Triggerfoot put it on straightaway with one-handed aplomb, gripping it at the crown, and smiled his broad handsome smile at Vermelle. His eyes flashed appreciation and joy.

Triggerfoot looked right in the hat. It was a perfect fit. The boys had taken care to get the size just right. *So that's what Beebo was doing with that piece of string 'round my head one evening when I'd nodded off a little in my chair,* Trig thought. When he woke that evening, they'd almost succeeded in trying not to giggle.

Yes, the boys might work out. They came from the old blood, and the old land, this very land too.

Then again, they might not. Triggerfoot had hope but was a realist also. Lads lacking the discipline of a workaday world brought up from a toddler's time might easily get bored. This short attention span and the need for variety and excitement, stimulations of every kind, was a thing that cities bred.

"Momentary men, " Mister Pink had called city folks. And that's where they'd lived. As a farmer, you had to take it for granted you'd have no options, no choice but to work, and just do the routine, grinding it out day to day. If you had to grit teeth in the grind, then grit teeth you did. No, they'd never been brought up to that, as he well knew, never to the downright grinding nature of farm chores.

Like most folks these days, they'd probably never seen any work through from start to finish. Men today only did partial jobs, a piece of an assembly-line process, and their minds were geared that way. As for farming, like making a crop, or a basket or chair by hand, you saw things through. It was a totally different mind-set and way. Trig thought to himself that this was another reason he wouldn't move to the gnat-span focus of the town. Too partial, too fragmented, fractured, a whole different sense of time. He liked the satisfaction of taking things through from start to finish. It was the pleasure of creation that a disconnected piece of a doing could never give.

Vermelle's boys. City boys, but they were Mister Pink's grandsons too, and they'd shown the right signs. He'd just have to see. Time would tell.

Verta May was also marshalling into service, of all people, young Eugene. He needed to strengthen up on the place. And

Berry's daughter Emmalene. Vermelle's daughter Madge would keep Emmalene company and help Verta May with the housework and do some of the lighter farm chores—tasks that their mammas had done twenty and thirty years before.

Quite a summer this next year might bring. In the meantime, all five families would converge for a week at Christmas time to pleasure and work in preparation for a new year. The place had not had the prospects of such life in many a long year—in fact, long before Triggerfoot's time, and known to him only by tales from old-timers and his mamma and pa.

Trig wondered for a moment how he and Becky would stand come six months from now, and where she would be. But he tried to put such questioning out of his mind. As for himself, he knew where he'd hang his Texas hat and where he'd lie down. No momentary man, he thought to himself as he focussed on shutting up the barn stalls for the night, feeding Flag and Bossy, and bringing in the foaming milk pail. He had his hands full to get through the day. It was most too much for one, and if he weren't a strapping, hard-working young fellow, it couldn't be done. He couldn't do it alone otherwise.

As he walked through the back door of the farmhouse, he placed his new hat on the pair of deer antler racks he'd made for the wall. The hat gave him real pleasure as a hope for Mister Pink's old ragged-out farm. He looked out upon his own slow, wordless fields, now obscuring in the falling dark, and was already thinking of spring.

XXII

Winter

Now into the deep of winter, Triggerfoot was having to face the hard truth that Becky Sue and he didn't have all that much in common. She was gravitating more to the Glenns' beach house at Edisto. She loved the sea, and walking the beach. She liked the tourist bustle of Charleston, and he'd heard (through the grapevine again) that she was trying to find a job on the coast or in the city. She'd applied at the college in town.

The cold and wet of the weather had seemed to enter his heart; but he worked on steadfastly at the farm and put his energies there. In truth, the place looked shipshape good. His hard work showed, and his account books, if you could call them that, were well into the black approaching the end of the year.

The diamond engagement ring sat in its little blue velvet slot in the silver-coloured snap-top box, there on his bureau. The bureau's mirror reflected its facets as Trig looked across at it from his bed. The image didn't taunt him exactly, but it was a rejection and rebuff, and this he knew. It was a rejection of all that he was and stood for, and even of the soil he stood upon.

There were plenty of young women in the town whose heads turned to see him when he walked there. He was aware of this.

So Trig was coming to see that there were more women out there than Becky Sue. He had had to feel that way, for she'd, in the second week of November, finally given him a conclusive No.

Trig was ready for the answer, had prepared for that day, and said no harsh word—in fact, few words at all. No play of colour even lit his face.

Yes, he could turn heads. "I'm smitten!" one of the beauticians in town had whispered to a client at the rinse table, when she caught a glimpse of him walking by the beauty shop window in their full view.

"Sally, how his jeans do fit him just right," she said.

"And in the right places too," Sally replied. "I wonder what that Becky Sue Glenn could have been thinking of. But they say she'll be moving to a job in Charleston before Christmas time. She's always been a prissy sort—thinks she's too good for here."

"The more chance for us," the beautician replied, and several of the ladies laughed.

But few women seriously entertained the idea of becoming Trig's farm wife. They'd become too used to comfort, and the convenient life in the town. And for them convenience also included not getting their new slippers wet and dirty by getting off the concrete or onto unpaved soil when they went to pick up the paper on the sidewalk every morn. They wanted to be close to the K-Mart and the picture show. And this Triggerfoot knew as well. He'd had a good introductory lesson in Becky Sue Glenn.

As for him, Trig was learning that contentment was not the fulfillment of what he craved, but the realisation of how much he already had. Some may not have thought he had anything, but he knew better. At times, when Becky Sue was off his mind, he felt this contentment fully. He didn't feel fractured, like so many folks in Clay Bank seemed to.

Trig saw that the Glenns, all of them, Becky included, hurried too much, rushing around always, like most of the business set in town.

"But Trig," Becky had asked just the other month, "don't you want to get somewhere? See more of the world? Do more things? Really make something out of yourself?"

He didn't know how to answer her. He'd never thought in that way. *What's the use of hurrying to get somewhere,* he'd thought, *when I'm already where I want to be?*

Maybe it was the discipline in his family for a century or more of not being able to buy pleasure, or to purchase leisure, that had developed Trig's capacity to enjoy to the fullest the things not sold in the marketplace and of not having to rush to get there to buy them. Happiness simply had nothing to do with that. On that truth, he and Mister Pink had always agreed without having to say a single word.

Perhaps it was because their world was close to Old Stephney, and they had lived in her shadow of want, and seen it at close range, that it was difficult to impress Trig and Pink with exterior things. They'd often found from experience that life plays the damndest pranks and likely as not bestows its richest material blessings with a lavish hand on those they would pity, and often gives, oh, so grudgingly, to those they were disposed to envy outright.

The Glenns always spent several weeks before Christmas on vacation at their Edisto beach house, so he'd not have to see her about town during that time. Just a glimpse of her there sent his heart racing and brought back the deep feeling of loss in his gut. His stomach would tighten to the hardness of rock, as if he was in the extremity of physical pain.

He could suffer that kind of pain, but this, this he didn't know if he could take.

By Christmas time, the Glenns came back, but without Becky Sue. She had taken a job at the main Charleston post office, the great ugly granite pile of a building at the corner of Meeting and Broad in the bustling centre of town. He'd seen it on his senior trip, and had thought it looked for the world like a prison, or imprisoning fortress, and now it was. Now he thought it a castle in whose tall tower his princess was locked away, and he'd have to hack his way through the overgrown briars and fight off the new dragons of the day to achieve her release.

But no, the difference was this maiden didn't want rescuing. She liked the bondage within. She liked castle towers, gilded cages, pavements, the glitter and glare, and the bustle of women and men.

It was a fair city, among the finest creations of human hands, and she was the fairest of fair, leastways to him. Perhaps she deserved to be in that faraway enchanted land. Perhaps it deserved to be graced by her blue eyes and lovely smile.

All he knew now was that the castle that kept her indeed had its moat, and that for him, the drawbridge was up and ever would be. He'd try to forget her and go on with his life. That's obviously what she had done, and had advised him to do. She had said she hoped that they could still be friends. To that he had said nothing, turned his back, and walked away.

He had never once given serious thought to moving to Charleston. "I'd rather be a hound dog and bay at the moon from my farm than be the richest, most famous man in that place," he'd declared. "This Brer Rabbit won't ever be happy except in his own briar patch. Just give me the hills and the rivers. None of that sand and flat land for me. Marshes are good for crabs and such, but not for old Trig and his kind."

So the grapevine had spread the word among the female population there, that young Trig-Tinsley-the-Handsome was free once again. This caused a few hearts of the fair sex to skip a beat.

In just whose, Triggerfoot had a pretty good idea, but having little vanity in his makeup, it didn't affect him much.

He stayed at his chores and his work, minded his business, and kept to himself. He hunted with Towse and old Bleat and lived with his memories with the land all around in a rich inner and outer world. It was here he would heal.

Yes, gored severely, he'd heal. Most things did. That was a lesson the farm had taught him, a lesson he didn't get in town or in school. Contentment seemed to settle on him like the fragrant pine needles that drifted to the forest floor.

One thing from school he recalled from his history book. It was an ancient marble statue of a wounded warrior. The Dying Gaul, it was called. He sympathized with the fellow—in fact, looked a lot like him too. When the teacher said that the unlucky man probably had blond or red hair, being from Celtic Gaul, Trig looked at him like a brother. He'd often return to the page where the statue was, no matter what section the class was on, and gaze, and try to ponder the man's thoughts. *Wonder what it would be like to be in his skin,* Trig often thought.

Now, he determined he'd be the dying Gaul revived, come back to health and life, freed from out of the marble to fight another day.

Becky Sue had cut him down, but he wasn't dug up by the roots. His stump would heal and grow another tree. His downcast eyes had looked up to the sky. Like the fallen king of Daniel's story, he praised his Maker and was made whole. Pink had often told Trig that story, and the lesson wasn't lost on him.

He kept remembering how with all Mister Pink had

lost, his friend never dwelled on what he didn't have, but on all that he did. And these were plenty enough. He sure missed his friend. He knew that his own lesson of contentment must have come at least partly from him.

Triggerfoot thought about what Mister Pink's children were doing over there at his place. So far, the sisters had been saying the right things.

It was Vermelle, surprisingly, who had taken the lead in proclaiming right off that they'd have to see how the land "carries itself" before they'd make any change. Their pa had learned how the place had borne weather and time, and they'd start with his choices of what to do and not to do, of where to do it and where not to. In this, they'd honour both their pa and the place.

At Vermelle's comments, Verta May and Mamie Lou had looked up from their ham and grits a little surprised. When Mamie Lou recounted this to Triggerfoot the next day, he was pleased. Richly pleased. He'd learned from his own father and Mister Pink that you took land as a process and not something static to be forced, or quartered out on a grid or balance sheet. "Land is life and energy. Like a river, it's alive," he said back to Mamie Lou. "And not something just to be eaten up. You give it your energy, and it gives back."

This left her about as amazed as when Vermelle had made her comments at breakfast yesterday. The world around here was full of surprises, it seemed.

"Food for thought," she said to Trig as she took her leave. "Yes, Katie Scarlett," she mumbled, "maybe the only thing that lasts and matters is the land." She smiled but was serious too.

Trig's visitor had left and he was musing too. *If torn, it heals,* he thought.

Mamie Lou had been the only person he'd seen in eight days, and he welcomed her stopping by.

He went back to his walk toward the barn, chores to do, things to be put straight in order, just to be disordered on yet another day, or maybe even before this one was through.

"Only you got to give healing some time, without being torn some more," he said to the dark empty air in the barn. The air was close and warm and smelled of seasoned hay and richness of animal breath.

"People tear and get torn nowadays too fast to be healed. And before they're healed, they're torn again." With his steady, patient nature, he'd not make that mistake.

XXIII

Christmas at Mister Pink's

~⌘~

Verta May drove down from Washington in the first week of December to get the place ready to receive the whole family, or at least to house who could or would join them there. Mamie Lou and little Goldie came down about the twelfth. She'd taken her yearly week's vacation and her week at Christmas time plus several days of annual leave to be able to stay close to a full month and help Verta May. Little Goldie was so bright and so far ahead at school, the teacher had given Mamie her assignments and said, "Go!" As usual, Byrd was travelling in his job, on the West Coast right now, but would join them soon as he could. He wanted to be with them and not in California—"the Left Coast," as he called it, "the land of fruits and nuts." He wished he'd not ever have to return there; but with his job, he knew he would, and soon.

It was Mamie Lou and Goldie who had charge of the tree and all the decorations. Goldie, who'd already learned her grandpa's woods pretty well, knew where the hollies with the best berries were, and she brought limbs of them inside. She put sprigs everywhere—on mantels, on windowsills, behind every picture on the walls. She twined smilax vine over the front door.

There hadn't been a tree in the house since well before their mamma had taken the cancer and died. And then, it had never had lights, just homemade decorations from the hands of the girls.

Mamie sawed down a nine-foot, fragrant, well-shaped cedar from off the place, which like most of Upcountry Carolina, had an abundance of them. This is the tree all of them in the community were used to.

"Y'all want a cedar, don't y'all?" Verta May had asked.

"'Course," they all agreed.

One year, Mister Pink had cut a nicely shaped pine, but they all said it wasn't the same. Next year, back to the cedar they went. The smell of the cedar to Verta May and Mamie brought old times rushing back.

"Funny how smells do that," Verta May had remarked. "They take you back in time quicker than anything. The old boxwood does that in the sun, and the gardenia and tea olive too."

None of them had thought to bring a Christmas tree stand, so they did the way their pa always used to do. Mamie nailed a cross piece of slats to the tree's bottom and put it in a foot tub, which she filled up with rocks and sand. This way, they kept the tree watered well, so it would last into the new year.

Verta May had a long string of multicoloured lights

she'd not used for many Christmases now. These, she had thought to bring, hoping they might have a tree like her mamma did many years before. The lights had been bought for her considerably smaller D.C. apartment-style tree. And though they looked a bit skimpy on the largeness of this one, they shone festive there in the great hall.

Through the wavy panes of transom and sidelights, the lights cast a prism-like diamond's glow.

Verta May had replaced Mister Pink's rags stuffed in the door's sidelights with glass pieces cut to her specifications in a glass cutter's shop in D.C. This was a wondrous improvement. She'd put them in herself in a matter of a day.

One of the rags that she removed, she recognised right away as a part of a print dress her mamma wore, about the time of Verta May's graduation from high school. She showed it to Mamie Lou. No doubt her pa had thought of his wife with some feeling too, as he placed it there. So for him, the rags were memorials, remembrances, as well as a way of keeping out the cold. The way the women did with quilts. They were entering their pa's mind.

Another of the rags was Verta May's own. It was a floursack summer dress she'd worn in grade school. It had yellow and blue roses in its design.

She'd not thought of it in years, but the sight immediately brought back a complete intact world, one that had been dead a long while, but in this miraculous way, waiting to resurface in time. She recollected the first day she wore it to school and how proud she was. She could see the back of the boy who sat in front of her and the whole schoolroom.

Still another scrap she recognised as Vermelle's handmade flour-sack blouse with the double frills. Their mamma was good with the needle and the old worn-out Singer sewing machine. This blouse was Vermelle's favourite, as Verta May recalled, and she knew her sister would welcome the sight of it again. She couldn't wait to show it to her. How pleased she'd be.

Then there was the ragged tail of one of Berry's shirts. It brought back his broad smile when he wore it in the ninth grade.

Yes, she was seeing into their pa, into the windows of his mind, in a way she hadn't thought to before. So the rags were not just randomly chosen, but carried memories in their stitches and folds. He'd not forgotten them, not a one, not a single day, as they may have him. He'd had them with him each day in his own way in the rags at his door. Each family member was represented there in his humble shrine, to the casual passerby, just an eyesore.

Still, as much as the fragments of cloth spoke of Mister Pink and their lives, Verta May knew they had to be removed. She didn't however throw them away. Instead, she carefully folded and put them away in tissue paper in the old pine blanket chest at the foot of the hall, now empty of Mister Pink's clothes. Maybe the time would come when they'd have, with her sisters and her sisters' own daughters, a big quilting bee.

She'd just the other day discovered her mamma's hand-made wooden quilting frame in the falling-down barn. It must have been a century old.

Then, like their mamma before, they could pass on these fond memories in the bright-coloured squares, shards of a shared life, again pieced back together as cover to keep out the cold.

It would be a guard against forgetting too, a talisman against the anonymous, the abstract impersonality of the time. As they quilted they could teach the young ones about old times and people they'd only know through their stories and tales. As they quilted, they'd talk and remember, tell tales. That way their blood would be kept alive.

Verta May could see the quilt pattern they'd choose, not the drunkard's path, or the six-pointed star, not the great tulip quilt, or the oak leaf design, but the great interlocking circle of wholeness, of things brought back together, united complete. She remembered her mamma had called it "Unbroken Circle," like the hymn they'd sung at her funeral.

When she mentioned this quilting project to Vermelle, they agreed that they'd do it. Just give them time. This, they wouldn't forget. Vermelle liked the idea a lot and said she'd make this her project next fall, the usual traditional time for the communal event.

Mamie Lou and Verta May had remembered to pack a few ornaments for the tree from their own stock and store.

These they supplemented with homemade things as they did in years before.

Little Goldie strung some popcorn and bright red holly berries to make garlands, and brought in a bird's nest from her growing rambles in the enfolding woods. She made red, green, yellow, and orange paper chains out of construction paper and glue. Goldie wished she had the other cousins to help her with this, especially Emmalene, who was her favourite, and still might get to come. The others would be coming in soon.

Goldie's own sister Dinah, who now had a brand new baby boy, would be joining them in just a few days, as would her father, Byrd, who'd cancelled a final appointment in Manitoba to drive down three days earlier than originally planned.

Truth was, from the conversations he'd had with his wife, and the joy they communicated, he was looking forward to the trip. He was a bit curious to see what his wife had done. His interest was piqued. Byrd made good money travelling the continent (the U.S. and Canada too) so had not thought twice about letting go the $13,000 Mames (as he called her) needed for her share of the purchase.

Byrd and Mamie Lou knew that they and their children paid a personal price for their bank account by his being ever on the road. And at first he'd not minded the airports, taxis, rental cars, and hotels. It was kind of exciting, an adventure, this seeing the world—back then. Now it had most definitely gotten older than old.

Mamie Lou, at the Enoch Pratt Library, had a full career of her own. She loved her job. The bright old building filled with its treasure appealed. It held a treasure of words neatly lined, and she was a proud keeper of them there. The ones who really suffered the most, of course, were Goldie and Dinah, but at least now Dinah had a husband, and at age eighteen, a child to focus her life upon. She had vowed to raise him at home. Her husband Biv had agreed that if she didn't want to, she'd not have to take a job. Doing a good job with a family was best job of all. And she was so young, really not much more than a child herself.

"This is fixin' to be one full house, y'all!" Verta May declared, as she looked up from her work at the stove. She straightened the red headrag on her forehead with the back of her hand. It was her mamma's. She'd found it in the top bureau drawer, where Pink hadn't touched a thing.

The old wood cook stove was baking and boiling to capacity as it had years before. The two iron pots of rice and turnip greens from Pink's winter garden were kept handy and full. Both Vermelle and Verta May were excellent cooks with the old staples of the place. They still hadn't wanted to graduate to quiche, deli trays, and melon balls on toothpicks.

"Full. Shorely is," Mamie Lou returned as she began to set the table.

They still hadn't been quite sure how all of this would turn out—or if there'd be quite enough room in the house.

"Bless our hearts! May be mayhem and bedlam besides,"

Verta May added with a shake of her head and a smile. Beads of perspiration from the heat of the stove shown on her forehead beneath the red headrag. For all the world, little Goldie told her she looked like the black lady on the pancake box.

At this, Mamie Lou and Verta May had a hearty laugh, and Mamie gave her a squeeze and straightened the shoulder of her dress.

All but Berry and his children were planning to be there. He and Sandra and his beleagured family were still caught in the throes of divorce and were buffeted by this storm.

That meant Vermelle, her husband Dawk, and three of their chaps—Danny, Beebo, and Madge; Richards, his wife Marissa, and Eugene; Verta May; Mamie Lou and Byrd with Goldie, Dinah, Biv Sr., and now baby Biv Jr. too. That made fifteen. Emmalene, if she could get down from Detroit on her own, would top out at sixteen.

One of the first things the sisters did after closing on the house, that is, after the kitchen was set right, was to open up several shut rooms that hadn't seen the light of day or felt the press of foot since their mamma had taken ill and died.

There were four bedrooms more or less in service now, and the second parlour could double as another during this time. This still left the drawing room, the great central hall, and the kitchen as communal gathering places for them all. With the stack of their mamma's quilts, they'd make pallets for the youngest children in any convenient spot on the old foot-polished floor. The crib and high chair Mister Pink had made, and that all the children had used, were discovered in the corncrib and would be put in service once again.

Any overflow that felt the need could always commute to the motel in town, but Verta May wanted to make it comfortable enough so they'd stay home.

"Home," she liked the sound of the word. She turned it on her tongue like the finest wine. Indeed, the point was to gather as one as a family in a true home, as their old pa had wished.

"Honour thy father and thy mother: that thy days may be long on the land which the Lord thy God giveth thee," the Good Book said. "Better late than never, I reckon," Verta May added her own line.

Mamie Lou and Goldie put the tree on the old pine cooling board at the foot of the great hall. Five months ago, Mister Pink's wooden box had lain there.

The ceiling ran to twelve feet, so the tree just fit. The cardboard and tinfoil star little Goldie had made touched the ceiling boards.

The tree's coloured lights were their own resurrection of sorts, marking the birth of a child that would end all death, darkness, and loss.

It was the season of promise, of faith's renewal. Life out of death, it was this that moved man—the symbolism of Christmas at the darkest time of the year, the season of solstice, the shortest day, the longest night in the new calendar year, the return of light and life.

A bright leading star lit up the void. It came to rest over

an humble place, maybe even humbler than this, a poor thrown-away place on the edge of the world to bear forth a king the likes of whom no powerful city or empire had ever seen. And a king who'd speak Aramaic, a provincial dialect that would like to bring scorn from the high and mighty of the land. And in the town itself? None knew the treasure that lay beneath the star.

The mighty wise men would come and the shepherds too. Pink had spoken of that to Trig just the Christmas before he died. In the old man's wisdom, he'd said he really didn't care much for the wise men but took the shepherds to heart. They were farmers like Trig and himself. And Trig had agreed on his choice. Awful wars had been the inheritance of the century; and Trig, in his own wisdom, had added, "Shepherds don't make wars." At that, Mister Pink had added that it was the shepherds, good ones at least, who gave us the best pattern for the Lord.

For the sisters, they were understanding full well now, that here on the land and in this place, it was not so much a standard of life to be spoken of, but a standard of faith. It was their Southern way with black and white alike and constituted a strong bond.

This year, Mister Pink's family had its own newborn too, Biv Hodges Jr., Pink and Goldie's first great-grandchild. He'd be here too in his own swaddling clothes.

"Those swaddling clothes better be flannel," Mamie had cautioned Dinah. "Be sure to bring warm clothes. No central heat here."

Triggerfoot was sad that Mister Pink had missed hearing of his great-grandson's birth by only a few days, for Biv Jr. was being born near a thousand miles away in a Baltimore hospital the very day before Pink's funeral. It may very possibly have been that Dinah's cries of pain in delivery came at the same time of Vermelle's own wrenching cries at her pa's cooling board. Verta May wondered about that.

In just a week now, Dinah and Biv Sr. would be bringing the baby to his people's home, a home its own mamma didn't know very well. The sisters had scrubbed up the crib and had it ready in Dinah and Biv's room.

Triggerfoot hoped Mamie Lou would take Dinah and little Biv down to the new healing mound, its red gash of clay already settling and darkening down with the cold winter rains. He knew that by next year at this time, it would bear its own bright emerald cover of moss.

XXIV

Tomorrow

From all accounts by everyone assembled and some who were not, the December gathering at Mister Pink's was a great success, the first that the folks there declared would, God willing, only be the beginning of many to come. They had plenty of food, brought in and raised on the place, but Mister Pink's smokehouse provided the crowning glory—hams that were as good as he and Goldie had ever cured.

With Triggerfoot's help, Danny had learned to take a rack of glistening honeycomb from Mister Pink's bees without endangering the hive or himself. With hot biscuits, this was a special treat. Mister Pink's pantry yielded up Goldie's pickled okra, canned beans, soup mixture, fig preserves, scuppernong jelly, blackberry jelly, and watermelon rind preserves. Some jars still bore their mamma's neat printed labelling.

The cousins had gotten on well. Emmalene had been successful in making the scene, to the great joy of the cousins, especially Goldie. Vermelle had picked her up in

Columbia off of her flight from Detroit. This time, the children had brought their favourite pastimes and toys. They learned to share and exchange. Little Goldie even led them on walks along deer paths she'd discovered in the woods. They brought in some more holly from their rambles to make two big wreaths for the front doors.

During their stay, Danny and Beebo went out several times with Triggerfoot, Bleat, and Towse on a hunt. Beebo had killed his first deer, a nice ten-point buck. With their usual good manners, the boys called Trig Mister Triggerfoot, as he called their grandpa Mister Pink.

Triggerfoot let them take old Bleat back home to Mister Pink's and keep him with them while they were there. This, he did, despite knowing the sad parting he could predict when the lads had to go.

On these hunts, Triggerfoot had killed a wild turkey and two deer, one a twelve-point buck, "a beauty" he said pleased, and the boys were good help in the bleeding, gutting, and dressing. They learned fast, Triggerfoot could see. He sent the dressed turkey home with them to their mamma.

Triggerfoot had the lads over to roast up the choice parts of venison, and, truth to say, Danny and Beebo would have followed Trig every step that he took and even slept there on the floor, if they and their mamma hadn't had better manners, and moderated their stays.

"Mister Triggerfoot, can we he'p?" they would ask. Or "Mister Triggerfoot, does you mind if we go?"

They loved everything Trig did, especially the juvenile

little funny jokes that he made. After a bigger than usual dinner, Trig needed to let one rip. He backed up to the fireplace of his old farmhouse, kind of bent over, and accomplished the mission, using the draft to do what drafts do.

"Mister Trig fartin' up the chimney," Beebo grinned. "Now I'se done seen everything."

As Vermelle said, as the family had been leaving to return to Houston after Pink's funeral, Danny and Beebo had sure taken to their friend Mister Triggerfoot. In fact, the word she used was "adored." This embarrassed the boys.

As far as Trig was concerned, Danny and Beebo were a welcome way of taking his mind off Becky Sue. And he liked the lads, their modesty and good manners, their quiet attention, their open frankness, and the quick way they had of picking up all that they saw. His Christmas would have been truly solitary without the Thomas boys. He missed Mister Pink, and he wondered if, at Edisto and the festive season in Charleston, Becky even thought of him. He struggled unsuccessfully not to think of her.

And Vermelle had invited Triggerfoot over to their big Christmas supper laid out the length of the great hall. It was some chilly there, but the good cheer of the company and a bright golden Christmas day sun had warmed things up. The temperature had reached into the seventies by mid-afternoon.

As Trig approached the great cirque of white oaks, glistening gold with mistletoe, he noted that the resurrection ferns on their giant limbs made a blanket of rich green.

There had been rains the preceding days and fogs and mists aplenty this December. Today, a great thick fog had covered the early morning sun. So the ferns had soaked up the moisture to the saturation point. Great water drops still hung to the splayings of their fronds like miniature full moons. These too were coloured gold by the sun. The branches of the rowan trees had a sunny glow.

Trig enjoyed the supper a lot, but, as was his custom, didn't have too much to say in a crowd.

Danny and Beebo sat across the table from him, and Vermelle noticed how they watched every little move that he made—the way he picked up his fork, the way he laid down his spoon. Vermelle declared that if they were around Triggerfoot much longer, he'd have himself two clones. At the incongruity of that picture—blond Trig and coal-black Danny and Beebo—both Trig and the boys had to laugh.

Triggerfoot said nevertheless that he didn't know two more clones (or was it clowns?) that he'd rather have. The lads were pleased to the tips of their toes. Like Triggerfoot too, their faces and gestures were perfect registers of their feelings about things. They were as frank and open as the sky and, if you were attentive, you could read them better than books.

Yes, Trig thought to himself, *they got their grandpa's honesty.*

Triggerfoot was coming to grips with his losses now, and would face the new year with hope in his heart. It had been dried out like those ferns on the great oak limbs, but was now livening again. He was glad Mister Pink's far-flung, fractured family was finding common ground, most literally, and had come home. He knew from farming that cooperative ventures were more successful than competitive ones. He just wished Mister Pink could be there to see. *Or maybe he was,* Triggerfoot thought, *in ways they could never know.*

At least for a time, Old Stephney was turned out of doors. She had no plate at the table there. She was around though, Trig knew, maybe at the edge of the dark woods, biding her time. She walked there from tree to tree, looking their way, as if waiting her chance. It was the natural way. But for now, he'd forget her. If he'd had his fiddle, he'd have taken it off the wall, and struck up a lively jig.

With a light heart, he listened to the three sisters' plans to put the place back in order. For the most part, they made good sense, and he gave advice on some points, but only when he was asked. Mainly though, he didn't say much, and though he didn't say so, he was deeply pleased. He didn't have to; they all could tell. Most of them had learned to read the rise and fall of colour in Triggerfoot's face.

When Vermelle recalled what her pa had said many years ago, Trig coloured for sure. "Pa always declared that in farming, like in all things, there ain't no shortcuts to success." She also remembered her mamma's "Good things are tough and need sweat."

Verta May recollected Mister Pink's lessons on rushing and taking shortcuts too. "They all run to loss," he'd say. "We're not in a race, not even with ourselves."

Trig thought, *Yep, cooperation, not competition, that was best,*

and what the world had forgot. If any success could come from this
undertaking, that'd be the only way.

Verta May had concluded that this was the way of their
people on the land, and not seen in the confines of her urban
career. There, competition was the expected norm and
encouraged too—the American way. But she was Mister
Pink's daughter; she hadn't been brought up like that; and
even though she could play the game as well as any of the
rest, the game had gotten stale and old, and was still a game,
a playing at life. It didn't please her at all anymore.

Cooperation. Yes, that was the satisfying key. Triggerfoot
had said true. And all manner of reconciliations too. That
was Mister Pink's way, the Tinsleys' way, the way of most of
the people around these parts, and now hers too. To the out-
sider, it might look like just good manners; but Verta May
was learning that it went deeper, far truer to the heart than
that. She had begun to think of her sophisticated D.C. circle as a false community held together by what Kierkegaard
called a common aesthetic damnation, a death that mas-
queraded as life. She didn't know it, but she and Trig had
come to the same conclusion about culture and how it
might be defined and passed on, and Trig had never even
heard of Kierkegaard.

During the conversation there at the table, Dawk and
Vermelle said that at one point they might try to move
back home, if not to the old place, then at least close by.
They'd be Triggerfoot's farming neighbours too.

Dawk said he'd like to try his hand and back at farming,

at least part time. Triggerfoot said, "Mainly back and tired legs and shoulders too."

Dawk reckoned he could find a janitor's job at a plant somewhere around here. Today, there were industrial operations all over—dotting this Piedmont landscape—disfiguring it, as Mister Pink and Triggerfoot would say. There were more and more complexes with every year now, and fewer and fewer farms.

For all his fancy title at the Aerospace Centre, a janitor was still a janitor, no matter what he was called. Dawk, like Vermelle and Verta May, had bedrock honest good sense, and didn't need titles, so, yes, old Dawk called the job what it was. A janitor he was, though highly paid.

As for the three Thomas children, they were ready to move, especially, of course, Danny and Beebo. "Tomorrow, Dad," they plead. Vermelle and Dawk hadn't ever seen them eager for anything this way. Dawk felt that this might just be what the kids needed. He and Vermelle were becoming increasingly alarmed by what they saw in the teenagers who went to school with their children.

There was no hurry at the table. They sat there talking quietly, sipping tall glasses of tea, and anticipating the feast to come. For now, their feast of words was enough. It had grown full dark. Trig could see that outside a fog had rolled in. It was turning much cooler by the hour, and the weather had all the signs that in a day or so, there might be snow.

"Falling weather," Mister Pink would've called it. Trig had noticed as he approached the old house this afternoon that the smoke from the chimneys was settling in low places, lying horizontal on the scene. Verta May sat at the head of the big Christmas board, the giant cedar tree glowing behind her. She looked down the table at sixteen faces of her kin, from Vermelle and Berry, the oldest there, to Dinah and Biv's new Biv Jr., not yet six months old, a range of half a century—to be precise, fifty-two years. All seemed relaxed and at ease, as if drawn into a fold.

She had no husband or child, had turned forty-five the month before. Her biological clock had ticked out, but here today at this golden moment and in this familiar place, she felt nothing missing in her world. Some people stayed single, she'd come to realise. It was that way sometimes in the world.

But solitary she wasn't, not here and with her kin, and with all of her blood gone before. Her mamma and pa, her grandparents too, were out there on the bluff looking eastward down to the river. She was in a place all of their eyes had regarded, loved, embraced, and taken deeply in. They'd looked at and accepted the very same mysteries of this particular land.

Home. Yes, home, she thought.

In the Tinsleys, and now Triggerfoot, they were lucky to have good neighbours besides; and as all in this community knew, the right sort of real neighbours was as good as family.

Triggerfoot knew that too. He'd help them whenever he could, and he knew the road went both ways. Verta May and Vermelle realised that he'd had a hard trio of losses, and they'd give him help and friendship when he needed. They didn't worry about him too much, though, for they knew there were young ladies there in town who'd be only too ready to console him. As short a time as they were there, they'd overheard bits of girl talk in town.

Verta May, with her family's help, and with Triggerfoot's advice when they needed it, would make this thing go. In some ways, asking Trig was almost like asking their pa.

She already had her plans for the spring ploughing, maybe reclaiming an extra few acres of prime, fertile bottomland that had been taken by weeds. Triggerfoot had tipped her off on the location of that.

"Maybe crowder peas," he'd said. "If you can keep the deer out." And that's what she'd try. She always liked black-eyed peas and Hoppin' John. She missed it in fact this Christmas time and would have it next New Years. It brought luck and good fortune, all the old folks in the community always said, like cooking collards to serve with the peas. Collards for greenbacks in the new year; peas for silver.

In the farming, Danny and Beebo were keen to help. They wanted to learn. Even Eugene was a part of the scheme. Only Richards, his father, held back. After all, in his career, as he thought, he had the most to lose, having climbed so far. He fell too intently and squarely into the big business world, but to his credit, wished them all well. The wish was sincere, and his sisters could tell.

Now, Verta May thought, if the Thomas five would only move there. That would nail down the future, if nailed down any future could be. She herself had put up savings from her salary enough, so that if need be tomorrow, she could walk clean away from D.C. Turn her back and not look behind.

She'd really not leave much that would last there or anyone grieving her loss, she well knew. There was really nothing or no one she'd miss. No, like those around her at work, if she left, she, like they, would have no regrets. They'd just interview, have committee meetings, and get some new eager young careerist at a lower junior salary to take over her job. "Let the competition begin again," they'd say.

Everybody would be happy that way. It was comforting to know that she'd have that option to leave, and there'd be no pain with the breaking away. Would she stay at her job? Would she go?

Right then, she honestly didn't know. Time would tell. It always did. Of that one thing, she could be certain sure. For a while, she had gotten outside time, with her life in D.C. Now, she'd gotten back in. She had bathed herself once again in time's flow, like the living river close outside down the hill. And she liked the swim.

"Time," she said out loud as she was cooking over the stove this morning. And repeated it, this time more clearly, "Time."

Vermelle, standing by her, asked "What? What time?" and got no reply.

For this was a part of Verta May's innermost, secret world, a word that she'd only just allowed herself, and she wasn't yet ready to share it with even those closest to her, not even Mamie Lou and Vermelle; no, not even they, at least not just yet.

Triggerfoot surveyed the gathering at the long table that stretched before him with perhaps the greatest pleasure of all who were gathered there. He needed desperately to see new life spring out of loss and decay. His world was a world of ruins, with everything he valued and held dear knocked about, gone to smash like a shipwreck on rocks, and the remnants warred still further against by the battering of waves, hour after hour, relentless, day after day. Still, he would stand there fighting the waves till breath was no more.

All of this had finally soaked deep into the very marrow of his bones. Even at his young age, in this respect, he was older than many grey-headed men. That was the world he'd been born to, like Mister Pink and his neighbours and farm friends. He figured rightly that his choices would not be the ones that would let him ease comfortably along. He'd already seen that with Becky Sue. He knew that for better or worse, he'd always be going against the grain, setting his body against some deluge of incoming tide, with some imaginary sword fighting the waves. He'd always be the odd man out. He'd reckoned that he'd always been anyway.

He was already marked that way—a country boy in a city world. He didn't think how he'd manage as the world got more citified and grew further from him, and he'd have to cope with the knowledge that he was getting more and more different every year. There were already more questions than answers, and the questions grew more numerous, and his answers got fewer every day that passed day.

One thing, however, he did know now more fully than ever before: that his own life lay with the land, this particular land, and the lessons and wisdom in its silent furrows and folds. The town, all towns, near or far, seemed even farther away. As long as Becky stayed in Charleston, her face too would recede and grow dimmer until at last he could no longer see.

The new year approached with its fresh, bright child's face, and, indeed, as he said to himself under his breath, with a hope born out of ruin, "Yes, tomorrow. A new start. A new day. If only the good Lord will help me along."

As he thought of the new year's promises, Trig exhaled a deep sigh, as if emptying stale air from his soul.

Verta May had graced the food. She prayed the right prayer of thanksgiving. To that, they all, Triggerfoot among them, said a heartfelt "Amen," and then just as fervently and devoutly, "Pass the baked sweet 'taters, Triggerfoot's venison steaks, and Pa's ham."

Later that night, with a stiff wind from the west, and Orion the Hunter in the sky for company walking home, Triggerfoot reflected on and rehearsed the scene that had just unfolded, and that had included him. In embracing it and making it his, he'd alter only one or two things. Mister Pink would be at the big table's head and would smile his broad honest grin as he passed round the food. None of the food would come from the store and all from the place. Yes, that was the improved, perfect memory

Triggerfoot would enshrine and keep, like another stronghold of a castle, not easily assailed.

More and more these days after his breakup with Becky Sue, he had taken to making a world in his mind, a world of certain reconciliations, convincing himself of that world, creating a place he could live. That was how he'd get by. He already had his castle, humble enough as it was, and in need of a good coat of paint; but that, as he knew, was more than a start. Like his pa used to say, he could also declare that what he stood for was what he stood on.

And in that knowledge, Trig's contentment grew. He was blessed in so many ways with his farming partnership with the Maker of all, and trusted that the pay, though not counted on for each Friday, would always be there constantly when he needed it, in the right way, and at the right place and time.

But, yes, it was more than pay and partnership even— a covenant more like, a reconciliation and bonding to the world.

Christmas. Yes, a time of, as the old carol went, God and sinners reconciled. Trig was coming to feel, as his father had before he died, that modern times, in discarding their way of life that touched the essential harmony of things, was breaking the most basic, the most fundamental covenant mankind could recall, and with that breaking, no holding together could remain. The world split, fractured, pulled apart. Trig took pride in the fact that for this betrayal, he and his people could not be blamed.

He'd also begun to learn that no day really comes back again. He already understood, as his father had always said, "An inch of time is worth a foot of gold."

So he treasured the meal that had just occurred as the right, oldest celebration of man with man. It spoke indeed of reconciliations of all kinds. Putting your feet under the table with your neighbours meant you trusted and welcomed them in the hospitality that was as old as man. "Community," what a precious fine word. Things held in common. The important things.

As he walked home alone, his strong stride suggested the rhythm of the Dave Coe song he'd taken to singing to himself more and more these days, altering the lines to suit his situation. The words dealt with having a .410 rifle and a bowie knife too, Red Man Tobacco that he liked to chew, and counting the cars when the train went past, and if that ain't country, you can kiss *my* ice.

At this changing of "I" to "you" and "your" to "my," Trig smiled a satisfied smile, as if he'd just finished some nasty chore, and his eyes danced with mischief.

The rhythm of the song and his powerful stride, coupled with the brisk cold air with a hint of coming snow in it, made his lungs feel clean, caused him to breathe so deeply that his chest swelled. The buttons on his camo jacket stretched about as much as they could without popping outright. The night gave him a river's flood of happiness. The stars were so bright and the air so fresh that he couldn't help but feel good.

But then the Coe song soon gave way to the few words of a prayer Triggerfoot had for some time been making up in his head. He worked it around and finally uttered it to himself, satisfied with it at least enough at last to let it go heavenward: *Lord have mercy on us, and save us from ourselves.*

And that about summed up Trig's current attitude toward the world.

His prayer went on its way, and so did Trig. As he often did in the depths of winter, when his footsteps greeted his own familiar fields, he turned his thoughts on this quiet night to ploughing, seeding, calving, and the fresh new morning light of spring.

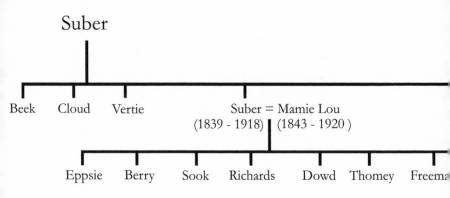

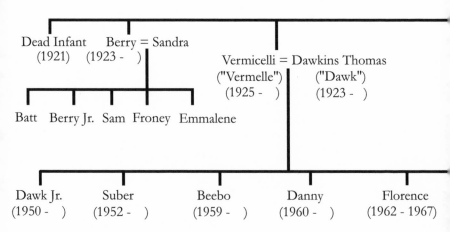

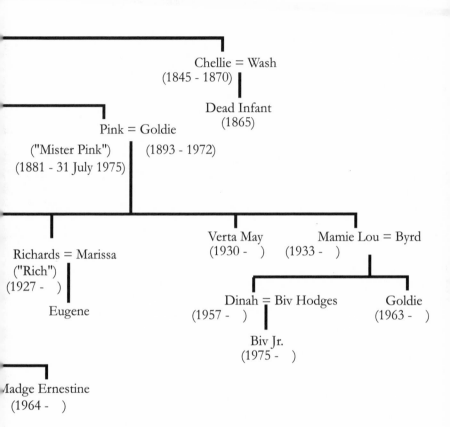

Chellie = Wash
(1845 - 1870)

Dead Infant
(1865)

Pink = Goldie
("Mister Pink")   (1893 - 1972)
(1881 - 31 July 1975)

Richards = Marissa
("Rich")
(1927 -   )

Eugene

Verta May   Mamie Lou = Byrd
(1930 -   )   (1933 -   )

Dinah = Biv Hodges   Goldie
(1957 -   )   (1963 -   )

Biv Jr.
(1975 -   )

Madge Ernestine
(1964 -   )

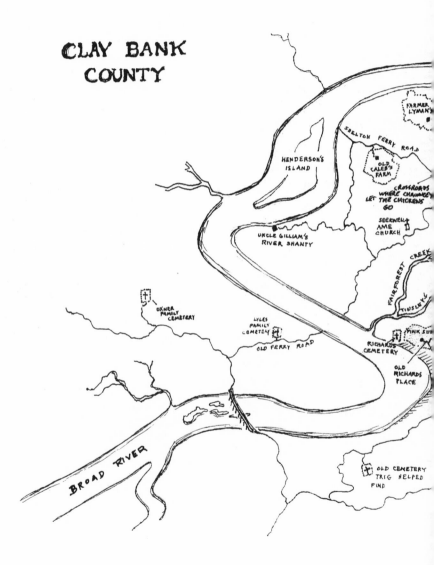

CLAY BANK COUNTY

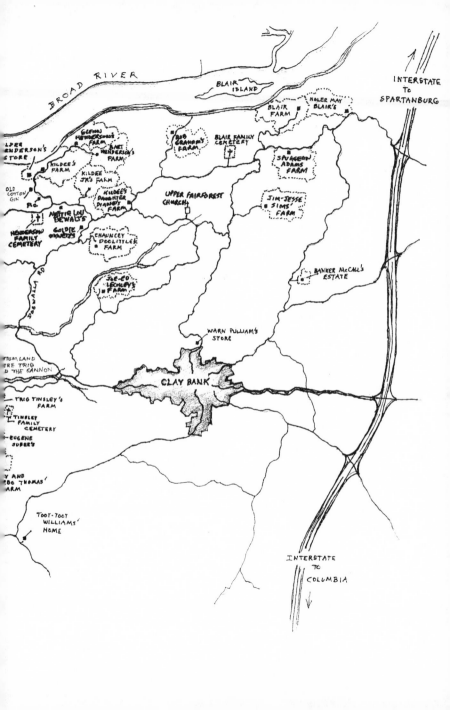